MICK. Born a blue-ey[...] [...]knit Irish community [...] [...]out for him. But what if it's a [...] he has no stomach for? Can he tear up the map and throw it away?

SULLY. He's always been Mick's best friend. He's always followed Mick's lead. But now their checkerboard neighborhood is changing, and Mick is moving off the white square of home—into dangerous territory. Should Sully follow? Does he really want to?

EVELYN. She's beautiful and she's a poet. She's also as hard as nails. Mick can't resist her—probably because he's the last thing in the world that she wants.

TOY. He's street-smart and worldly-wise, and nobody messes with him—ever. Mick can't believe how lucky he is to have Toy as a friend. And then he begins to learn some of Toy's closely guarded secrets. . . .

TERRY. Mick's big brother is a violent drunk, and an even more violent bigot. In fact, he's the local hate monger. Lately he's been hating the fact that Mick doesn't want to follow in his footsteps. . . .

Also by Chris Lynch

Shadow Boxer

"A gritty, streetwise novel that is much more than a sports story." (Starred review)
—*School Library Journal*

"The fight sequences, fraternal dynamics, and memorable cast of eccentric characters make for some riveting episodes in this rough, tough-talking book about boxing and brotherhood."
—*The Horn Book*

Iceman

"Much better than the usual sports novel, this is an unsettling, complicated portrayal of growing up. . . . A thought-provoking book guaranteed to compel and touch a teenage audience." (Starred review)
—ALA *Booklist*

"Hockey enthusiasts will enjoy the abundant on-ice action, although this novel is clearly about much more. . . . *Iceman* will leave readers smiling and feeling good."
—*School Library Journal*

Gypsy Davey

"The dialogue crackles with realism . . . in terms of literary quality, this work is outstanding." (Starred review) —*School Library Journal*

"Young adults will appreciate [*Gypsy Davey*'s] honesty and fast pace. Lynch steers clear of sensationalism and paints characters who ring true every time."
—*The Bulletin of the Center for Children's Books*

Blood Relations

Blue-Eyed Son #2

CHRIS LYNCH

HarperTrophy

A division of HarperCollins*Publishers*

Blood Relations

Copyright © 1996 by Chris Lynch

Library of Congress Cataloging-in-Publication Data
Lynch, Chris.
  Blood relations / Chris Lynch.
    p.   cm. — (Blue-eyed son ; #2)
  Summary: Uneasy with the drunken violence and prejudice of his brother and others in his Irish neighborhood in Boston, Mick makes friends with a somewhat enigmatic Spanish-speaking loner at school.
    ISBN 0-06-447122-5 (pbk.) — ISBN 0-06-025399-1 (lib. bdg.)
    [1. Prejudices—Fiction.   2. Irish Americans—Fiction.   3. Boston (Mass.)—Fiction.   4. Alcoholism—Fiction.]   I. Title.   II. Series: Lynch, Chris. Blue-eyed son ; #2.
PZ7.L979737Bl   1996   94-18728
[Fic]—dc20   CIP
                                            AC

Typography by Steve Scott

1   3   5   7   9   10   8   6   4   2

❖

First Edition

Contents

Part One

A New Game - **3**

Out in the Sun - **26**

Hang Fire - **35**

The Grip - **50**

El Micko - **67**

Augie's Dogs - **87**

Brother Love - **109**

Part Two

Refugee - **129**

Cambio - **148**

O'Asis - **168**

Table for One - **193**

Hermit Crab - **209**

Part One

♣

A New Game

Family was my problem. Not simply the obvious problem of *who* was in my family—my brother, Terry—but the whole idea of family itself. Where I come from, it's a big word, *family*. You hear it a lot in my neighborhood. And it means the neighborhood as much as it means actual blood relations. It includes the guys you grew up with and the guys your dad grew up with and the girls they hooked up with and the kids they all squeezed out. It wasn't all important that everybody in your "family" be all Irish; you could throw in a little Pole here, a little Goomba there, without it mattering too much, as long as they lived inside your boundaries and acted like you acted and were Catholic. What family was, mostly, was what it kept out.

But the new thing I was learning was that family was as hard to get out of as to get into. All the old jokes were coming too true for me: You can choose your friends, but you can't choose your family; Family—can't live with 'em, can't shoot 'em.

Maybe they couldn't shoot you, but they sure could break your head if they wanted to.

When I opened my eyes, lying there on the sidewalk in front of Evelyn's house, the first thing I felt was confusion. Could this have happened? Could I have gotten my ass whipped just because I wanted to visit this particular girl, and because I was walking with that particular guy? Everybody has these scary, violent dreams, I told myself, but then you wake up sweating to find that it wasn't real.

Or you wake up bleeding to find that it was.

Some of the blood was already dry when I reached up and touched my eyebrow lightly. Something was dripping, though, new and cold, dripping on my head. I looked up. Evelyn was standing over me, a sandwich bag full of ice hanging from her hand.

"You've been bleeding up my sidewalk," she said, pushing the bag at me.

I sat up and took the bag. I didn't even try to talk yet as I pressed the ice that felt so good into my crackling skull.

"This like an elephant thing or something, where you wander off looking for a place to die, and you pick my house?"

I could die now, I thought; I at least got her talking to me. She made me smile, even if she didn't make herself smile. Not much ever did make her smile, actually.

"You going to live?" she asked.

I gave it a little thought. "I'm going to live."

"Fine." She turned and walked away.

"Wait," I yelped anxiously, hurting my head in the process.

Evelyn turned, arms folded. "Why?"

"Because," I said, trying to think of why she should. "Because I'm your guest. I'm in this situation because I was coming here to see *you*."

"You were coming here?" she asked sweetly, "to see me?"

I nodded.

"I don't recall, did I invite you?"

How mean could she be? For how long? Even

5

blood wasn't good enough for her. She didn't wait for a response to that last one.

When she was gone, I sat there, my legs splayed out on the sidewalk in front of me, the ice melting in my hand but pleasantly numbing that corner section of my brain.

It's not like I've got anything more to lose, I thought, climbing to my feet. I trudged slowly up the stairs and rang the bell.

The door opened. "Yes, who is it?"

It was Ruben. "Goddamnit," I said, delighting him.

"Hello? Who is it, please?" he asked, looking past me. "Is there anyone there? Hello?" He stood on his toes to look over my head, then back down to look left and right, like I was invisible. "Hello, is there anybody out there?"

I turned around and walked back down the stairs, back toward home.

Maybe it was blood loss. Maybe it was the numbing effect of the ice, slowing me down, chilling me dead, taking away the pain from my head and now taking everything else with it. The small patch of temple gone dead with the cold, then the feeling spreading until my whole skull simply teetered up there like an empty shoebox.

Everybody else in the neighborhood seemed to have the deadness too. The eyes I met on my slow serpentine weave down the sidewalk showed me nothing. Nobody showed me any pity, not that I should have been looking for any. But nobody showed any surprise, either, at what must have been a pretty gruesome sight. And nobody showed any smartass, good-for-you sucker kind of pleasure that you might have expected. *Nothing.* No thing. Smaller than nothing and farther away than Jupiter, that's what I saw they saw when they saw me. The high school kids I recognized, nothing. The couple strolling past me, licking ice cream cones and pushing a baby carriage together, nothing. One giant four-generation family massed on the front steps of a yellow triple-decker, nothing.

Not that I expected love from these people, but I *was* looking for something when I took the trouble to look at them instead of at the ground. I mean, somebody should *notice* a thing like this, shouldn't they? *I* would, if it was me. I'm hurt, I thought, and I don't know if I will make it to the corner without falling and hurting myself more. I was walking sideways like a crab, dizzy and weak, and if I fell I would be left there on my face like a piece of garbage until I could get myself up and out by myself. Just then I got a picture of me like that, in my head, lying there alone, and I felt like I wanted to cry for him, for myself, the self I was watching there alone in a heap on the pavement.

By the time I turned the corner from Centre onto my street, Scotia, I'd regained some strength. I was walking steady now, but I still felt like I'd been hit by a car.

"What happened to *you*?" marveled Mrs. Ryan as she hung laundry on the clothesline in her front yard. Her clothesline in her *front* yard, like it's attractive. "Come over here now, you."

I went to her unquestioningly because I seem to automatically do anything I'm told by women my mother's age. She took my chin in her hand and yanked it side to side to get the best look.

"You're a good boy, Michael, so I know you didn't start it. I hope you got the better of it."

I shrugged.

"Try a piece of raw red meat," she said, turning back to hanging her bloomers in the breeze.

"I'll try a piece of red meat," I echoed, already walking.

"Boy's earnin' his stripes," Caughey called from his window, from where he watches every move on the street, every day, instead of working. The drapes didn't even part when he talked, just ruffled a little bit.

"Who gotcha, the spooks? The ricans?" said the guy they call Southside as he drove his wheelchair right into my path. He was always doing that, springing out from behind his wooden fence to surprise people walking by his house, like a bridge troll. "Here, have a pull, tell me about it," he said, shoving a forty-ounce, brown-paper-wrapped can at me. "Didja kick 'em in the balls? Kick 'em in the balls, is whatcha should do."

I did hear a few disapproving tongue clicks, indicating not everyone thought this was great. And just before I got home, I heard Mrs. Healy moan from her porch, as her husband leaned over his fence to get a gander at me, "The poor mother, she's just the sweetest creature on god's green earth. She don't deserve any more o' this."

"Ah, yer makin' too much outta this," her old man said. "Boy's cuttin' his teeth, establishin' hisself. You're the spittin' image a yer brother, kid, more like that crazy damn Terry every day." He laughed.

He thought it was a compliment.

Instinctively, as if I was smacking a mosquito, I lunged out and snatched him by his loose-skinned fifty-five-year-old throat.

"Stop that!" Mrs. Healy screamed, tripping as she hurried down the stairs, falling to her knees. Mr. Healy tried to pry my hands off but I had a vise grip on him. I was pulling him by the neck over his five-foot chain-link fence.

Mrs. Healy had gotten to her feet, her knees all scraped, and was slapping my arms. "Let him go! Stop it! Let him go!"

Mr. Healy was running out of fight, going purple and struggling less, when I turned to look in his wife's face. *Then* I heard her. *Then* I stopped.

Mrs. Healy wrapped her arms around her husband, hugging him, holding him up. I leaned into him, pointing, the tip of my index finger touching the tip of his needly nose. "Go to hell!" I screamed. I turned to go and saw a circle had gathered around me to watch. My neighbors.

I walked around the circle, sticking my finger in every face. "And go to hell. And go to hell. And go to *hell*," I said, to all the people who hadn't done anything to me. Southside. "Go to hell." Fat, flowered-dress Mrs. McMillan. "Go to hell." The impossibly ratlike, pointy-headed, wide-hipped, ten-year-old Mason triplets with their filthy freckled faces and too small clothes. "And *you* go to hell."

When I reached the steps of my own house, I dropped. I sat there on the bottom step, my legs stretched out into the sidewalk in front of me. The numbness from my head had spread, wending its way down and through me. I felt nothing everywhere. Did I just strangle somebody? Did a lifelong friend just crack my skull open?

Where was Sully? *Who* was Sully? How come he pulled out just before me and Toy got whacked?

Toy? Jesus, Toy. Did Toy make it?

The questions just rolled around in all that empty space way up there in my head. I couldn't answer them, couldn't get near them, couldn't hold one thought long enough to figure it out.

When I was in first grade I was out sick the day they took the class picture. They took my photo separately when I got better. The print came back a month later, an eight-by-ten, and everyone got one. There was everybody in my class huddled together, shoulder to shoulder, stacked in three rows. And there was me, a cutout, a small oval with my gap-toothed, crew-cut face, floating toward the upper right-hand corner, above and apart from the rest. The oval floating head.

That was exactly, *exactly*, how I felt here again.

Suddenly, Terry was standing in front of me, leering, taking me in in all my wonder, knowing everything by now of course.

"Fall down, little boy?" he chuckled.

I lifted my head. "I did," I said, almost as if this was a real conversation. "I fell in the forest, but nobody heard."

"Gee, that's a shame," he said, giving my head

a little sideways shove as he passed me on the stairs.

"Well then, you did have a big day for yourself, didn't you?" my nurse said with a little smirk.

I had just explained to her what I knew about why I was there in the hospital with a concussion and a cracked sinus. It got harder for me to detail it, the further I got into the story, because things kept getting fuzzier. I remember little after seeing Terry on the porch. I think my father brought me in, yelling about what I did to the neighbors. That was the big thing, for the nurse—how I got myself all smashed up *and* choked a guy in completely isolated incidents on the same afternoon.

"Have they got you on Ritalin yet?" she asked.

"Huh?"

"I'll mention it to your doctor," she said, winking.

"Thank you." I closed the bad eye so the good one could focus on her as she left. I was still trying to work it out when the nurse disappeared out the door and was replaced by . . .

I rubbed my eye.

She was replaced by . . .

I took the pills the nurse left me.

Evelyn. *The* Evelyn. *My* Evelyn. Heartless Devilyn Evelyn.

"You gotta be kidding me," I said.

"I might be," she answered. "Might be a hallucination. A medication thing. Or a conk-in-the-head thing. I wouldn't trust it if I were you."

"I won't," I said. I rolled over, pulled up the covers, and pretended to ignore her even though my blood was gushing so hard I was afraid it would come out all my seams. Thirty seconds into it, I sprang up in the bed, exhaling as if I were breaching from under the sea.

She remained motionless, leaning in the doorway, wearing a baseball cap. The blackness of her hair, the shiny satin of it, lay against the shock-white doorjamb, softening the room. "I heard the details," she said. "I also heard a rumor you're maybe not such an ass."

"Thanks."

"I didn't say I *believe* it. Just that I heard I should come see for myself. So far I'm not seeing anything convincing."

"You've been talking to Toy. Is he all right? How is he? Where is he?"

"I don't know," she said.

"What do you mean, you don't know? Did you see the guy or didn't you?"

"No," she said, and stopped. She was going to make me work for this. She was going to make me be nice.

"Please," I said more respectfully. "What's going on?"

"I don't know. Toy just called me up—which was strange to begin with, because he doesn't do that—and asked me to come and have a look at you. Explained a little about the mission you were on when you prostrated yourself on my sidewalk, and then he said good-bye because the pay phone was clicking and he was out of change and after he hung up the operator was going to call him back and he was going to have to walk away with it ringing at him and he hated that."

"So where was he?"

"I don't know. He wasn't in school today, either. But he said to tell you hi. He's a weird guy. I like him a lot."

"He is," I echoed, looking away from Evelyn to stare out my window at the other half of the sterile hospital building across the way. "And I do too."

The two of us sort of hung there silently for a while. I continued to stare out across the courtyard, looking hard to see if there was another me way over in one of the matching windows of the other wing, staring back to see me seeing him seeing me. I never did believe in that parallel universe business, but at the moment, I don't know,

14

it felt like it was there. Like I was out there, over there, or at least like part of me was.

"Look, I have to be going," Evelyn said, simultaneously bringing me back into the room and wrenching my heart. It dawned on me that I was blowing it, the grand, heroic, lying-in-the-hospital moment that girls are supposed to be crazy for. I wanted to get her to stay but in lieu of words I hyperventilated.

"You really were coming to *my* house, huh?" Her head was tilted way over to the side, still in disbelief.

I nodded proudly, dumbly.

"That's awfully sweet. Stupid and completely divorced from reality, but sweet anyway," she said, and reached into the bag slung over her shoulder. She pulled out two flowers. "I brought you a present, like you're supposed to when you visit somebody in the hospital. I brought this one, the lily, in case you were dead when I got here. And the yellow carnation in case you were better." She looked me over for a few seconds. Sighed a breathy sigh of indecision. "Here, take 'em both."

She placed the flowers on my chest, in front of my folded hands. Just like I really was a dead guy. She patted my hand and told me she'd see me around.

It didn't take much, did it? I smiled up at her like a baby, felt something warm and spikey expanding through my chest near where she touched me. *Barely* touched me. When she'd left, I quickly turned to try to catch a glimpse, a peek of the other guy just like me who, I was feeling sure now, was over there, staring out his window. I wanted to see how he looked *now*. But I couldn't find him, so I turned back and grabbed the hand mirror off the wheeled tray table beside the bed. I was going to see this, this happiness thing, at its peak, to see what it looked like.

That's not what it's supposed to look like, I know that much, I thought as I looked at my face. The part that's supposed to be flattened out, between my nose and my cheekbone, was all swelled up, as if my nose were not growing out of a regular contoured face but just stuck onto a big bumpy round surface like Mr. Potato Head's nose. My eye was half shut, the inside glistening with healthy shiny new blood, the outside black. A big letter C of slashes curved around from over my eyebrow, down along the side of my face, and hooking back in under the cheek. It did not, to me, look at all like me. I could not take my eyes off of it.

I buzzed the nurse. "My head's really hurting me bad now," I said. Then I looked back down and watched myself, or whoever's face that was, talk to her. "Could you get me something? I really need something." I felt very sorry for the wreck I watched in there. I would definitely have given him something.

"Well, you aren't due for anything for another three hours. All I can give you in the meantime is a couple of Valium. You want them?"

"I want them," I said. I watched my face say it, and with every syllable, with every second, that face seemed further away from me, seemed less me. It wasn't the first time I'd looked in a mirror and hadn't recognized myself. But it *was* the first time I wasn't sure the feeling would go away.

I didn't look at the nurse as she placed the tiny pills in my hand. There was something like a numbness, and like a supersensitivity in my palm at the same time as her nails lightly scratched it. The other painkillers were actually working just fine. She left. I took the Valium, sat back against the propped pillows, and stared some more.

"One punch," I marveled. "All this from one punch. Is my face that soft?"

"You're too damn soft for this," my father said as he wrestled with the steering wheel. Terry let him have the truck to pick me up. I'd been released, after thirty-six hours and one visitor, with a bottle of pills and instructions not to operate heavy machinery, drink alcohol, or blow my nose.

"You're not the man your brother is, Mick, so maybe this fightin' stuff all the time ain't for you."

"Maybe it ain't, Dad," I said, smiling out the passenger window. " 'Cause I sure ain't the man my brother is."

"And I promised old Healy you'd apologize for stranglin' him, so you *will.* I explained to everybody that you was mental from gettin' beat up, so while you still ain't none too popular with the neighbors, nobody's pressin' charges."

It was true that I was mental. It was also true that I was sorry for choking old Healy—but only because it made me look even *more* like Terry. But it was also true that if Healy told me today that I was just like Terry I'd probably choke him again.

"Okay, thank you," I said, because right now I simply wanted to get along. I was humming along fine. My painkillers were killing my pains. I'd just had a little vacation from *everybody.* And I was under medical orders to do nothing but lie on my back for the rest of the week. I wasn't happy, exactly, but I wasn't not happy either, which was good.

It was supper time when we got home. I popped a pill before walking in. Already seated at the table were Ma, Terry . . . and Sully. In the middle of it all was a meatloaf that I could tell from the doorway was about eighty-five percent Bell's meatloaf mix, with a lit candle in the middle of it.

"Welcome home, sweetheart," Ma said, a little teary, a little tipsy.

"How come you didn't come and see me?" I asked before taking another step inside. I hadn't planned that question, didn't realize it was even in there inside me. It just blipped out when I laid eyes on her.

"Well . . . well, your father had to work late . . . and early . . . and I couldn't get anybody to take me . . . the visiting hours over at that crazy hospital . . . I tried, god, did I try to get over there. . . . "

"Okay," I said. She only leaves the house when my father takes her. I blew out my candle, got instantly dizzy, and slumped into my seat.

Terry got up, took the keys from Dad, and left. He was only waiting for his truck.

Dad sat down with his rack of beers, and helped himself to six or seven slabs of loaf and a big ladleful of water-logged diced carrots, all perfect little orange squares. Ma served me, but I didn't look down at the food. She served Sul, and he dug right in. He hadn't even spoken to me yet, the rat. I watched him chomp his first few bites. He could feel me watching him, I knew.

The meal went on in perfect, typical, blissful silence until I broke it up.

"Please excuse us," I said, kicking out my chair and pulling Sully, still chewing, up out of his.

"Oh, you don't like it," my mother pouted.

"No, I like it just fine," I said. "It's just, you know how it is, that fine hospital food's got me spoiled."

She nodded, relieved, humming her agreement with her mouth full. "Ummmm, ahh, that's true. I had such a salisbury steak the time I had the kidney stone out . . ."

Sully wasn't too happy, because he was hungry. But I'd make it up to him. I pulled a couple of beers from my father and headed off to my room. There I shoved a can into his hand, put some ancient, spacey Pink Floyd on the stereo, and whipped out my medicine.

"Meds?" Sully said, wide-eyed and stupefied. "They sent you home with a whole bottle? Didn't give them to your father? They left *you* to *self-medicate*?"

I didn't quite see the joke. "Ya, so what's so amazing about that?"

He laughed, pulled back. "Nothing. I just thought of something funny, that's all. Has nothing to do with you."

"Good. Here," I said, and stuck two pills in his hand.

He looked in his hand, looked at me. I ate my pills and swallowed long on my beer. Pink Floyd swirled all around the room.

"I feel funny," Sully said. "This is weird, doing this kinda shit at home, with the old Mom and Pop gumming away on the meatloaf one room away."

"So?" I said.

"So, it feels creepy, that's all. It's like inviting your parents to a circle jerk. I mean, it kinda spoils the atmosphere, y'know?"

"Hell, what are you talkin' about, you never did no circle jerkin'," I said.

Sully was indignant. "Sure I did. It was with the Boy Scouts. We were at a jamboree with this scoutmaster who was in the seminary over at St. John's, and he's playin' his guitar, and we're all sittin' around the fire and he breaks into a round of 'If you're happy and you know it, pull your whang—' "

"You did not, you lying sack," I cut in.

"Okay, I didn't. But I thought about it. And when I think about it *and* add my folks to the scene . . . *brrrr* . . . well, it's totally blown, all right?" He stuck the pills back into my hand. "Here, knock yourself out."

I stashed them back in the bottle. We both polished off our beers, and when I heard my parents leave for the O'Asis, I went and got us more. We sat at the kitchen table.

"Sully, what happened to Toy?" I asked in a way that let him know I wasn't playing.

"I don't know," he said, shrugging.

"Did you know they were gonna be waiting for us?"

"I don't know."

"What the hell does that mean, you don't know?"

"I knew the *when,* all right. And I told you guys that. Your brother told me, and Augie told me, and Baba told me—they're all tellin' me at the same time, get the picture?—they told me *when* it might be a good time not to be with you guys. And then I risked my life tellin' you and Toy. But you wanted to be *brave.*"

Sully could say the word *brave* in a way that made you ashamed of it.

"Coward." I grabbed his beer away from him. "I ain't drinkin' with you."

He grabbed it back. "Bullshit. I was still *there,* wasn't I? Right up to the last minute. I was ready to hang in there. You don't know, Mick, I was standin' there, tryin' to be cool, hopin' they were just bluffin' and that they wouldn't do it, but all the time, I was pissin' myself. You know, that brave shit ain't my bag."

I got cooler yet. "So then, *where were you*?"

"Well . . . then, then Toy started with all that secrecy jazz, y'know, the Spanish. I didn't know he was no Spaniel. You didn't neither, don't lie. And then, y'know, I didn't know what to think. I was thinkin', Well, who the hell *is* this guy, anyway? I don't know jack shit about him. He's hidin' stuff from us and . . . who the hell knows what's up with him? So I was pissed, maybe I'm not exactly sure why, but I was. And I figured, screw this, I ain't gettin' my head caved in for *him*. What would I have been fightin' *for*, if I hung in there?"

He looked at me, expecting I don't know what. A nod, or a smack in the mouth. But I wasn't giving him any. "And me, Sul? What about me?"

"Mick, I swear, I never thought in a million years they'd pull any real shit on you. I still can't believe it. I guess . . . I guess the rules've changed."

"Playin' a new game, Mr. Sullivan. The rules have changed big time." The way I said it, and the way I just let it hang there between us, Sully knew that I was sort of putting it to him, a question, a need for him to declare.

"You know, Mick, I don't mind that Toy's . . . that he ain't in the family. I was just surprised. He's just so shadowy, he makes me nervous. I need to know things, you understand that."

Again he waited for me to lighten his load. Again I didn't.

"I heard he got away fine. Not a scratch."

I didn't even blink.

"I'm a go-with-the-flow kind of a guy, Mick. This against-the-grain stuff is hard for me, doin' things different than I usually do 'em."

"So it's hard for you, Sul. I know that. So what's wrong with hard? What if I tell you I'm gonna be an against-the-grain kind of a guy from now on? What're you gonna say to that?"

He stood up, paced. Finished his beer and got us two more out of the refrigerator. He sat down close to me, almost touching me, but not touching me. We don't do that. "I say, that's really hard for me. I say I don't know what I say. I say gimme a pill. But just one."

I smiled and threw the pill in his mouth like I was feeding a fish chunk to a seal. We drank the beers down.

"Come with me," I said, and the two of us wobbled down the hall to Terry's room. I pulled open the top two drawers of his dresser and pulled out every one of his precious collection of pocket T-shirts. I gave Sully the neat little stack of navy blues and yellows. I kept the three different shades of green. Sitting cross-legged on the floor and using Terry's own Swiss army knife, we took turns cutting the pockets off all those shirts. It was like gouging the heart out of some game animal.

We fell into a laughing jag as we did it. In the end, as we stood over the dead pile, I said to Sully, "He never, never leaves the house without one of these stupid damn things on. So now, he'll never leave the house again. Thus, we have already made the world a better place."

It made perfect sense at the time.

Out in the Sun

Something happened to me when I attacked Terry's shirts. I woke the following morning bold as a blue jay.

"Nice shirt," I said to Terry when I saw him later that day. He was wearing one of the navy Ts, with a second one turned inside out underneath to cover the gaping hole in his chest. He didn't say anything back to me. I knew he wouldn't. One thing you could always count on with dear Terry was that he couldn't remember half of any previous evening. And while my own recall was pretty shabby, I retained just enough to enjoy the hell out of this. He was always doing pointless, idiotic things under the old influence, protesting something—gays in the military or an IRA bomb that failed to kill the Brit it was meant for—that he could never recall or care about again. And I knew he thought he sliced up his own clothes and now felt like a schmuck.

"Fall down, didja there, Terry? Good thing you had two shirts on, huh?"

"Wanna be dead?" he growled as he grabbed his coffee to go.

"Better dead than red," I said. I'd been waiting all my life to say that to somebody. But he wasn't even listening anymore. He slammed the door in my face.

Cock o' the Walk, I had no school for the rest of the week, and a doctor's note in my pocket to prove it. Sure there was a little headache to go along with it and the occasional oozy discharge from a stitch, maybe some dizziness, but I had my medicine—now *there's* a thought—and nothing else but time.

I decided it might be fun to go to school. Not *to* school, actually, not inside, but there, around it. To see my babe.

"What are you, *nuts*?" Evelyn snapped. "Don't you ever, *ever* call me that again. Not even in your dreams. *How* hard did you get hit in the head?"

She had me so frazzled I thought it was a real

27

question. "It was kind of like when a car falls off the jack—"

"It will feel like a powder puff compared to how hard I'm going to clock you if you ever use that sexist ignoramus crap on *me* again. You got that?"

I nodded, dumb as a bug. I felt my eyes blinking, beating like hummingbird wings. I didn't do it on purpose, but it worked in my favor anyway. She relented.

"So how are you feeling?" She scowled.

"My head hurts a little."

"Well, go home to bed, fool," she said. It wasn't unpleasant, and it wasn't totally cold, the way she pushed me around.

"Okay," I told her dutifully. "Will you come and see me after school?"

"No."

"But Toy told you to check on me, remember?"

Now she got truly concerned. "You've seen him?"

"No. He's still not around?"

She just shook her head solemnly, gave me a weak wave, and walked back to school.

Well, that's enough, I thought. This much I can do. And I walked to Toy's house.

I pushed the buzzer six times, then held it on

28

the seventh, all pissed off and adrenalined about I really wasn't sure what.

"Ya, ya, ya, YA!" The woman snarled as she ripped the door open. "What's your *prob*-lem, goddamnit?"

She froze me. I hadn't thought it through this far, to someone actually being there and answering the door, and it left me standing there with all my stupid hanging out. She looked down from the step above, thick peach-colored terry-cloth bathrobe hanging on her very loose, soaking up fresh shower water from her skin. A white towel twirled up in a cylinder from her forehead like a ten-gallon pillbox.

"Hey," she said, snapping her long fingers in my face. "I said, *what* do you want?"

After a few more mute seconds, "Toy," I blurted.

As I said Toy's name, the irritation ran out of her face. But it wasn't replaced by anything else. She folded her arms across her chest, breathed in audibly through her nose, and exhaled the same way.

"Toy isn't home," she said.

"Well, um, could you tell me where he is? I've kinda been wo—"

"No, as a matter of fact I can't tell you where he is."

She let that one hang there, even though it was obviously unfinished. Could she not tell me because she *wouldn't*, or because she really didn't know? The way she said it, kind of harsh and pugnacious, seemed like she was daring me to ask.

"I am his friend," I said. "If that's what you're worried about."

She gave me the tiniest little half smile, the same thing as saying "Duh" to me.

"I know who you are," she said. "It's not like you need a damn program to keep up with all Toy's many *compañeros*."

I got a little embarrassed, remembering the one time we'd met, when she had no shirt on. Suddenly, I could not shove that picture out of my mind, and it made it even harder to talk. "Oh, ya," I said, trying mightily to be as cool as I could, which was none too cool. "Ya, I believe, I believe, we did meet, I think I remember."

Her smile grew and became more like a real smile, less like a poke. "Yes, I imagine you do remember. What is it you want with my boy?"

"Well, I just want to check on him, to see that he's okay, that everything's all right." I stopped, looked for her reaction, but she didn't respond. She just nodded the way teachers do when they think you can do better. "I miss him," I said, and was amazed to hear it.

"Good answer," she said, turned, and walked back into the house. She didn't close the door, so I didn't go away. In a minute I heard her coming back down the stairs. She walked out onto the porch with a mug of coffee in her hand, strolled to the top step, and sat down. She'd left the towel upstairs. Now she shook out her wet head, letting her long, kinked, silver-streaked brown hair hang down to dry. It was one of those first good warm mornings of spring when if you stood in the sun sixty-five degrees felt like eighty-five, heating up your head and your still March-thin blood. "I like to let the sun do its work. Normally I blow-dry it, but when the sun is right I like to just put myself in its way and let it soak into me. My hair feels better after that, and it smells better, and I feel, I guess, cleaner. From the sun, you know?"

I turned my back to her and looked up into the sun, to check. It hurt my eyes. Always did. Damn too light eyes. I closed them, and it still hurt, right through the thin pink lids. But I knew what she meant.

"Ya, it feels good," I said as I turned around to look at her through the sun spots. "It does make you feel, I guess, cleaner is right. You feel kind of weird and kind of dirty if the sun is out and you stay inside all the time. I love the sun."

"Really? You don't look like it."

I looked down at my hands, white and dry as rice paper. "Well, I do need to get more of it."

She nodded, almost as if she wasn't listening, took a sip of coffee, and leaned back. "What happened to your face?" she asked, sounding like she already knew. Although everything she said sounded to me like she already knew.

I reached my hand up automatically, my fingers lightly touching and covering the bad spots. I had forgotten about them, and now I felt grotesque.

"Do I have to tell you?"

"Certainly not," she said, and kindly moved on to something else. "He goes away sometimes. Trips. He calls them just that, trips. His father calls them that too, trips. Captain Trips, is what I call his father, who also likes to go on trips. They go off together a lot of times. Alone lots of times too."

I nodded, because I was supposed to.

"Toy is not his name, you know, and I never call him that. That's just a stupid thing his father started calling him when he was tiny, because that's all Carlo thought of having a baby, was that it was like having a great toy around. His name, though, is Angel."

Whoa. Why did that change things? Of course I wouldn't know, but I did know that things *were* changed. Angel. Angel? God, there was so much more now. With him *gone*, there was so much more here, now. Somehow it felt more like I'd gotten inside him. I would probably never use his real name—he did call *himself* Toy, after all, and I wasn't about to mess with what Toy wanted—but it was *there* just the same, wasn't it?

"So then, is he gonna be here, you know, anytime soon?"

When I didn't hear anything for a few seconds, I looked up to find she'd been staring at me, distantly, dreamily. "Sometimes it's a long time. Sometimes not so long. But as he gets older, the trips get longer, and more frequent. I worry. It all scares me. Not like with Carlo, because who cares? But with Angel? It's very sad. And I can't touch him. He is a wonderful boy, and warm, but he's off by himself. And when he returns? He's gone, off even further. I cannot touch him. Not with words, and not with the mother's hands. I cannot touch him."

She wouldn't stop staring at me. I liked it. It made me uncomfortable. I wanted her to stop, but she wouldn't. I couldn't be there anymore, even though I decided I liked her very much, I could feel the time running out on this, running out on me as I got anxious.

"Well, okay," I said in a moronic, light, casual way, like I didn't come here for anything big in the first place. "I'll just try again, maybe next week." I stood, wobbled, started sidestepping away.

She stood, took a last gulp of her coffee as she watched me. "I have a feeling. I think Angel may be here tomorrow. Why don't you come back tomorrow?"

"Thank you. Okay, I'll try. Thanks again . . ."

"Call me Felina," she said, changing somehow with the distance, back into someone steely and tall and motherlike at the top of the porch steps. When she pivoted and disappeared back into the house, I fumbled out a couple of pills and ate them like Flintstones chewable vitamins.

Hang Fire

I spent the next day where the doctor, my mother, and even Evelyn said I should have stayed in the first place. Bed. Spring sprang full that week, the sun shone, and I hid inside. The sun makes me nervous sometimes.

Without dragging out all the gories, what I did was hang in my room, listen to music, and amuse myself privately. I was beginning to hear the footsteps that were the end of my medication run with no refills. The bottle that was supposed to last me two weeks, if the pain persisted, was two-thirds empty after three days. Shouldn't've shared 'em with Sully, was the problem. Or maybe rotten-ass Terry got at 'em. Not that he would eat them, hell no. He says that drugs are ungoddamn American and that all they do is pervert the experience of beer. What he would do instead is dump them down the toilet and leave me groping in the dark so that I woke up in the promised land with a pill bottle cap stuck in my throat.

So I slept with them under my pillow and worked it out so that I could make it on one pill every few hours and if I took it with a beer that I shot right down without breathing, I could achieve and maintain a certain precious state. Hold it for quite a while, stretch out the ride over my whole rehab vacation.

On Tuesday I listened to the same disc all day, *Out of Time* by R.E.M. *All* day. I put it in the machine in the morning and hit the repeat button. I counted how many times it played altogether, but then I forgot how many that was. Sully swears that R.E.M. and Pink Floyd are the same band. Maybe, but after listening to them however the hell many times, I don't think so. Just to be sure, I planned to listen to *Dark Side of the Moon* all day on Wednesday.

Wednesday is a total blank.

Thursday I listened to *Dark Side of the Moon* all day. It's a different band.

No idea how much time had passed, but

when the music stopped, I snapped to with my eyes wide again. *Sproing*.

"Told ya it was the same band," Sully said as he stood over the stereo. "But never play *Moon* while you're sleepin', it screws your head. You were screamin' pretty good."

I was propped up rigid on the bed, my arms extended behind me to keep me from falling back. I could feel my eyes wide and dry, the moisture from my eyes coming out on my forehead instead.

"Mick, you look like you don't know who I am," Sully said.

"I know who you are, numbnuts."

"There." Sully relaxed. "That's better."

"I was screaming?" I asked.

"Who the hell is Felina?" he answered.

"Shut up. How long have I been sleeping?"

"How should I know? What time did you fall asleep?"

"I don't know exactly. Afternoon. Three, three thirty."

Sully looked at his watch. "Seventeen hours."

"Cut the shit," I said. "What time is it?"

"Ten past eight. I just stopped to look in on my way to school."

"Eight? In the morning? It's not Thursday anymore?"

Sully laughed at me, waving me off like I was some big joker. "Pretty screwed, huh, Mick? I thought you had big plans for cuttin' back against the grain. You don't mind my sayin' so, this looks kind of like your old grain."

"Takes time," I muttered, slouching lower in the bed.

"Ya." He laughed. "I hear changing your spots can be a pretty tricky operation."

He had me beat. I lay there without answering.

"Who's Felina?" Sully pressed.

"She's my *mother*," the cold voice growled from the doorway.

Sully stood frozen, staring.

Toy stared back. With his arms over his head, his hands gripping the door frame above, he looked all spread wide, staring *down* on Sully, *bearing* down on him. Like a meal. The hawk and the squirrel.

"Holy smokes," I said, and leaped out of bed. My knees buckled and I got intensely dizzy, so I had to sit back down. Fell down, really, while the blood got back to all the needy places. "Oh god. Ouch. Oh god."

Toy walked into the room. He walked right to Sully, getting in real close, aggressive close, uncomfortable close. Ready to talk, ready to listen to anything having to do with the last time they saw each other. He made it so that, with Toy's chest in his face, Sully had to do *something*.

Sully's face turned red, his eyes turned down. "Glad to see you got away okay," he mumbled.

"Ya, thanks a bunch," Toy responded.

Sully left without a word.

When Sully left he grunted at something in the shadow of the hallway. Then Toy's other surprise stepped into the room. Evelyn.

"Jesus, this is a damn party," I said, excited and silly like a kid. "Where've you been, Toy?"

Toy was not at all excited or silly. "Where've *you* been?"

"The disabled list," I joked, still failing to read the mood of the room. "Evelyn, love, I knew you'd come back to me."

She shook her head and flared her nostrils in disgust as she looked me all over. "You know, you got a *boca loca*, boy. Every time I see you, you say something moronic to me."

"I'm stupid with love," I moaned.

"You're stupid with *something*, that's for sure."

I laughed, feeling it was a compliment of some kind, then looked up to Toy for him to share it with me. Toy had this way of showing his expression even while hiding most of it under his hat. And he was showing me something angry now.

"So where you been?" I chirped. "You look good."

"I was on a vacation."

"Excellent. Where'd ya go?"

"None of your business."

"Maybe we picked a bad time, Toy," Evelyn said. "We'll see him at school next week."

Without thinking, I reached for my pills. Toy snatched the bottle out of my hand and read the label.

"What's your problem?" Toy demanded.

I hate it when people ask me that. "Maybe she's right," I said. "Maybe you should go now."

"Do you know that it smells in here?" He leaned down into my face. "It smells like a toilet. Are you aware of that?"

"Well, I wasn't, but thank—"

"Jesus, Mick, are you sick? Where is every-body?" He stopped, reached down on the floor, and picked up a brown half-moon-shaped some-thing. "Jesus Christ, is this a *hamburger*? Isn't anyone taking care of you?"

"I'm not sick." Suddenly I felt defensive, angry. "They're all out working right now. Shoppin', maybe. My mother brings me in food. The other night my father asked me, from the other side of the door, if I wanted him to wheel in the TV for a couple of hours. So you see I'm taken good care of, thank you very much."

Maybe that was a good thing to tell him, because when I said it he stopped picking on me. He just sighed and slapped his thighs loudly with his hands.

"You really don't look well, Mick," Evelyn said, brushing past Toy. She came close and raised my chin with two fingers. She was so warm, not that she had any special feeling for me, but because she was one of those people who cannot ignore hurt things—even if she does try to make exceptions. She was so beautiful, she made me want to hurt myself.

"Can I have my pills back?" I said flatly to Toy.

He reached right over Evelyn and grabbed me. With his big hand he seized me by the neck, his thumb pressing on my jugular, two fingers squeezing, crackling the vertebrae in back. I let out a small scream.

"Toy, don't!" Evelyn yelled. She grabbed at his arm and I saw her nails sink into the underside of his biceps, the part that should be soft but on Toy wasn't. "You're hurting him, Toy, stop it."

She kept trying but he moved as if she weren't even there, dragging us both down the hall. When we reached the bathroom he shoved me inside, flipped on the light, and jammed my face into the mirror.

41

"*Look* at that garbage," he said.

I hadn't looked in a mirror in a while. Not since the weekend, probably. Not on purpose though—it just wasn't something I did very often.

My eye sockets were deep and black, my skin was blotchy, off-white, and chalky. My hair stood straight up in the air on the left side and in front, and lay pasted to my head everywhere else. It was all matted together in lumps and shiny with oil. My teeth were dark.

"Hot damn, I look like Keith Richards," I said, snarling and bobbing my head at myself.

"Fool," Toy snapped. "The right response is supposed to be 'Oh my *god*, I look like Keith Richards.' It's not really a good thing."

"Would you lighten up for once," I said, turning away from the mirror.

"You big spoiled baby," he said, blocking me from leaving the bathroom. "I finally realize, you have no problems that you don't make up all by yourself." He hesitated, his lips pulling in tighter, harder, as he struggled for words. He looked straight up at the ceiling, then back toward Evelyn, as if she could make it come out clearer. Suddenly his face whipped back around to me. "You have no right," he finally said quietly. "No right. You have no business. You have everything." He let me go and shoved me backward at the same time. "You make me sick." With that, Toy stomped down the hall and out of my house.

I was thinking about what he said, agreeing with him, but at the same time missing the pills he'd just taken away. As I headed to the kitchen for an eye-opener, I bumped into Evelyn. She had *stayed*. My heart started beating again.

"He's so intense," I said, shrugging.

She folded her arms. "I think it's your self-pity, self-absorption, self-flagellation, self-mutilation, all that self-stuff that Toy can't relate to."

"Huh?"

"Grow up."

"Oh. I get it." Not that I actually did. "Where was he all that time, Evelyn?"

She shook her head sadly. "I don't know. He doesn't say." Evelyn started walking down the hall toward the door, and I followed her.

"He certainly came back with a stick up his ass," I said.

She shook her head. "What is it like for you, to live every moment entirely beside the point?"

"You like me, I know it."

"Good-bye, *Boca Loca*," she said.

"Wait," I said as she started down the stairs. Suddenly none of it seemed funny anymore. I was very nearly alone. "Could you stay with me for a while?"

"No. I have to go to school."

"Oh," I said. "That's right, I forgot. I'll be going. Next week, I'll be going again." I was mumbling by the end of it, backing away from the door, thinking already about the refrigerator.

"Don't do what you're thinking about," she said, shooting her arm straight out from the shoulder and pointing at me. As if she knew exactly. It gave me a shudder. She sat down on the top step, and I came out to join her.

"I only have a couple of minutes, then I really have to go."

"I know. That's okay."

"He seems to really like you. Toy, that is. For some reason."

"I like that. I mean, even if he's yelling at me and calling me garbage, there's something I like about it."

Evelyn nodded, looking out at the street.

"How about you . . . Evelyn?" I asked as timidly as I could without snuffling around her ankles. "Could *you*? Do you think? Like me?"

She squared around to look at me. My heart sank as I saw my rotten face reflected back at me again, in her black eyes.

"No, I don't think so. I mean, anything's possible. But I don't think so."

She stood up, started down the stairs again. I

remained slumped on the step, head dropped, staring into my crotch, staring at the same cutoff denims and same yellow-white T-shirt I'd been wearing since . . . when?

"Maybe," she called back, snapping me right out of it, "I could take another look. *Maybe*, you could bathe. *Maybe,* you could get some vitamin A into yourself. *Maybe*, you could detoxify by the time school's out this afternoon . . ."

I jumped up and called, much too loud to be cool at all, "Maybe."

As she slinked that confident, slinky walk down the street, I grabbed my head with both hands. The jump had done the screwy thing to my circulation again, making me teeter. And I smiled so hard my dead face muscles ripped me with a sensational pain.

I showered with lavender soap, my mother's Jean Naté shower splash, and dandruff shampoo that felt like battery acid seeping into my scalp. I worked a big gob of some spermy hair conditioner through my hair, clipped my curling, doglike toenails, and baby powdered all my problem areas. I even shaved, even though I was a couple of weeks shy of needing to, just so she could see and smell the effort of the blood on my neck and the lime Edge gel in the air.

Two hours before school was out, I was ready, sweating, thirsty, my stomach all flippy. I sat, nibbled saltines, sipped ginger ale, changed my shirt twice, watched *Green Acres*, *The Beverly Hillbillies,* and *Andy Griffith*.

When Evelyn walked up to the house, I sat on the front steps shining dully like a pearl.

She laughed out loud.

"I'm goin' in the house, dammit," I said.

"No, no, no," she said, grabbing my hand and putting my little fire right out. "I didn't mean to make fun. I think this is nice. You do smell like about twelve different things, but each and every one of them is better than what you smelled like before. Truly, I'm moved."

Truly or not, I bought it. "Where should we go?" I asked.

"The museum."

"The museum? You're taking *me*, to the *museum*?"

"Well, I'm not *taking* you anywhere. I'm going to the museum, and you seem to want to go someplace with me, so there we are. You don't have to go."

"No, I want to, I want to. I was there before. Eighth-grade field trip. Had a swell time. It was colorful, I remember."

"Ah, yes," she said, smirking, "that's the place."

The museum looked like a neat clean prison, with its tall slitlike barred windows, concrete everywhere, flat roof where there might be armed guards planted on all corners. High above the main entrance hung a massive banner with pictures of round cupids flying over a sign that read THE AGE OF RUBENS. The cupids were shooting arrows downward, and my eyes followed, down to where the arrows would land, down to the broad front lawn of the grounds, where they would lodge if they were real arrows, which they weren't, and if the cupids were real, which they weren't, into the back of the crying Indian who lives there on the lawn on his horse. I pass that Indian a couple of thousand times a year and I look at it maybe ten. Because it does something to me and I don't like what it does to me. He has a full headdress on and it's falling down his back as he stares straight up at the sky. His hands are pointing straight down at his sides, his palms facing us on the street. He might be crying, which is why I call him the crying Indian. He might be screaming. He might be laughing, but he doesn't feel like a laughing statue. He might just be soaking up the rain, or the snow that lies on his naked arms so much of the year and makes me feel stung frozen and hollowed out just to look at him.

The Indian stood there when the big banner said RENOIR. He stood there when it said DEGAS. And when it said GOYA, and THE SECRETS OF THE EGYPTIANS, and EAKINS, and THE WATERCOLORS. But I never had even a little bit of interest in walking past the crying Indian to go see any of it.

I wasn't aware that I had stopped walking. "You going home, you staying there, or you coming in?" Evelyn asked.

It's different when you're an eighth-grade kid, though, isn't it? Everybody was stupid and ignorant then, so it wasn't a problem.

But it was a problem now. I couldn't go in there now, with Evelyn, and have her see. She belonged in there. I belonged out on the lawn with the Indian.

"To tell you the truth, Evelyn," I said, "I don't really go for angels that much."

"Cherubs," she said. "They're called cherubs."

Exactly, I thought.

"Right," I said. "But I'm starting to feel a little run down. Still recovering, you know."

"Oh," she said. "You going to be all right?"

"Sure, it's just, I just don't want to hold you back."

Evelyn nodded, I nodded. She went her way, inside. I went back my way. I spent a few minutes with the Indian before going home.

At least she got me to bathe.

The Grip

"**I** didn't even say thank you, for everything, the other day." I stood as frigid and lifeless and white as a snowman outside Evelyn's homeroom. It was Monday morning, my first day back at school. I'd only been out for a week, but it felt like Baba's big hand had knocked me into next year. Even the Friday afternoon I'd just spent with Evelyn felt already like another life, like something that couldn't possibly have really happened to me.

"What are you thanking me for?" she said, slapping the air between us. "You never even got past the front entrance."

"Ya, but," I lowered my head and my voice as

two girls passed by, walking into class. "You took me. You got me interested for a minute there. Hey, next time I might even go inside."

"How come I didn't see you be shy before?" she asked.

"Because, ah, because I'm not, that's why. Not that I know of anyway."

By then Evelyn's class had filled, as had all the others. As I stammered away a smallish fist hit me in the back.

"Hey zombie boy, welcome the hell back," Sully said.

Not that I wasn't happy to see him, but I was talking, or trying to, to *Evelyn*. "Go," I snapped, pointing toward the bank of pea-green lockers across the corridor. "Go. Wait for me over there. Go. Get over there, I said."

He went, and cowered from me like a gerbil in a cage.

I turned back to Evelyn. "Um, I was wondering if we might maybe actually do something now, like together. A date, maybe?"

She sighed, which didn't sound good, but then said, "I don't know . . ." which did sound good because of the way she let it drift off there at the end and because it was a whole lot more than I was expecting.

"We could do something, some kind of thing

that you like to do. But not like a museum or anything. Something more like a real date thing. Whatever, what do you like to do?"

Losing ground because of my mouth again. She frowned, at the museum remark, I think. "I don't like to do very much. I mainly lead a life of the *mind*."

She said the last word real pointed at me, like I couldn't possibly grasp *that*. I tried to consider all the possibilities there in that statement. It didn't sound good. "A life of the mind. You mean, *all* the time?"

She covered her eyes with her hand, headache style, but beneath, her wide wavy mouth was smiling into a laugh. "I hope these *boca loca* things you say all the time are on purpose, because if they are, you're the funniest boy I ever met. But if they are not . . . *dios mío,* we've got big trouble."

I was so relieved to see her laughing at me, I joined in. "Hell yes, I'm funny all the time." I turned. "Sully, come here. Tell Evelyn, aren't I funny all the time?"

"All the time," Sully repeated with all the humor of a state trooper. He didn't quite get my Evelyn thing. Evelyn didn't quite get my Sully thing, either.

The first bell rang, so we had to get to our classes. "We can talk later," she said.

"Excellent. Later, we can talk then," I called anxiously, like all this was all going to disappear if I didn't nail it down. Like a very loud public beg.

"You're embarrassing," Sully said as we strode through the door of homeroom. "I'm gonna fix you up with my sister."

I had to bring my absence note to the teacher, and Sully walked up to the desk with me. "Not Honey again, Sul."

"What's wrong with Honey?"

"Nothing's wrong with Honey. Shut up a second, I have to hand in my note."

The teacher, Mr. Gennatassio, Mr. G, if you were a jock, took my note without looking up right away from his newspaper. After reading the end of the article, his puffy lips moving slowly along with the words, he turned to my note.

"You were out a whole week?" he asked, closing one eye for extra puzzlement.

I shrugged. He shrugged. I went to my seat with Sully in tow. Sully sat right behind me, buzzing close into my ear.

"So what about Honey?"

"Nothing about her."

"So then you'll take her out."

"No. Stop it, will ya. You talk about her like you're lending me a baseball glove."

"Nah, she likes ya, I know it. And she's pretty available at the moment."

"She's eighteen years old, for god's sake. I'm fifteen, Sul."

"Kinda excitin', huh?"

"No."

"So you'll get together with her then, right?"

"No."

"Give 'er a spin. What do ya got to lose?"

"I got something, Sul. Y'know, I got something going here I think."

Sully stopped leaning close. He pulled back, reclining in his seat. "Whatsa matter, Mick, you don't like white chicks anymore?"

The loud bell clanged like a fire bell. Sully stood. I stood, wheeled, and blocked his path.

"First," I said through gritted teeth, "we ain't ever gonna have this conversation again—the color thing, I mean. Next time you open your fat mouth like that, I'm gonna close it for you."

He nodded, blinked about a million times. "You know I didn't mean nothin', Mick . . ."

"Second, I don't want to date your stupid sister because she's dumb, Sully. Okay? She ain't *ignorant* stupid, like yourself, I mean, she's decent

54

enough and I like her. But she doesn't have a fully working human-size brain either."

I turned and left him there, pondering. He had his pondering face on. "So? So what's that, a bad thing all of a sudden?" he asked, tagging along after me.

It was a pretty uneventful return to school. The day dragged on the way days there always did. But there were differences. I think my notoriety wore off while I was gone, allowing me to return to my identity of Mr. Nobody from Nowhere. Which I had missed. But the classes, the things the teachers were saying, the stuff that used to pass me by and not bother me at all, were now making me angry. Geometry, Western Civ, English. Were these dinks for real? I couldn't believe how much they were all *wasting my time*. Get your Romantic poets out of my face. Rhombus? *Rhombus*? Oh ya, there's something I'm going to bring home and put up on the refrigerator with a cheeseburger magnet to show to my family. Hey Dad, wanna see my rhombus? Revolutionary art—those unfinished pictures of old George and Martha again, some second-grade-looking painting of Crispus Attucks getting whacked at the Boston Massacre. Ooohh, I'm glad I made it back in time for all this.

Part of the problem was my concentration—I

was a little soft after lying around doing nothing for a week. But the bigger problem was the school itself. My school was old school. It was part of that whole scene—the neighborhood, the town, the people—that I wanted to change. It wasn't the school's fault, it was just that I wanted everything to be different now, I wanted to find myself in a changed world, and I couldn't get interested otherwise. How could I last another month and a half till it was over?

Which was why I got my first detention warning for falling dead snorting asleep during history class just before lunch. The laughter woke me up. Mr. Murphy had filled out the little yellow jug slip, rolled it like a cigarette, and stuck it in my ear.

I couldn't have jug. I couldn't spend an extra hour in school. Detention was one of those things I was determined to leave behind. If they put me in jug for five minutes past that last bell, I'd throw myself out the window. I was getting out, moving up, making myself better.

Which is why I groveled.

"It's my head, it's my injury, it's my medicine," the mention of which gave me a little pang. "Please, Mr. Murphy, it's just been hard for me to get readjusted, that's all. I'm still having nightmares. I've never been so upset. . . Please, I'll be better tomorrow."

I could feel the warmth of everybody's enjoyment of my ass kissing. Mr. Murphy certainly was basking in it. He wasn't one to tear up slips, but he was beaming over this. I think if he could get everyone to react in this degrading way, he'd happily replace detention with boot-licking. Anyway, I was free.

Yet I found that freedom was a relative thing: I had eluded detention; I had retained Baba O'Reilly. He was in that history class, sleeping *most* of the time without anybody sticking anything in his ear. He punched me a greeting as I slithered toward the cafeteria.

"You was out a week, loser? You lyin'?"

"Cut the shit, Baba."

"What shit? I didn't know you was out no whole week. What happened ta ya? Ya get wasted or what?"

I kept walking, but looked up at his face to figure out what he was up to. His face was, as usual, blank. He wasn't being funny, didn't have the knack. The truth was he honestly didn't remember knocking me out.

"You broke my head, you big fat load."

He backhanded me across the shoulder with

his big paw. "What? I never hit you ever, ya bony little rat. If *I* hit ya, ya'd *feel* it, I'll tell ya that."

"Duh. Like I didn't feel it, in the goddamn hospital. Moron. Just get outta my face."

I pushed through the big metal door into the cafeteria where a couple hundred students were already eating, the first of four shifts. Sully waved me over to where he was at a table on the far wall. As I slanted that way, Baba grabbed me and spun me around. "I don't get outta nothin' I don't wanna get outta, you understand me?" While he held my collar with one hand he snatched my brown-bag lunch with the other. He held it up in my face and squeezed, letting me watch as pieces of an orange, Reese's Cups, and a tuna sandwich pushed through the soggy bag and oozed between his fingers. "I'll kill ya. I'll kill ya. I'll bite yer pointy little face off. I'll kill ya."

His hard cheese breath was blowing in my face, making me squint. I didn't do anything. He wanted me to do something. There were things I could do. In the past I would have done something, a kick, a gouge. Nothing that would make me win, of course, but just enough to make a guy remember that beating my ass wasn't something you could have a good time doing. But I didn't, wouldn't do it. When I looked into Baba's sickening trog face up way close, I saw things. I saw my life pass before my eyes. Not the way people say they see it when they're about to die, which I may have been. More like, I saw myself from when I was in this situation before, or something a lot like it, like I had been many times. I saw myself act, and I saw myself lose. And I saw myself do it all again. So now I saw in Baba's familiar ignorant mush, and my pale reflection in it, a loser.

"That's okay, man, you can keep that. I was gonna buy the hot lunch today anyhow."

So that was my move, to just leave it alone. I tried then to pull away, to leave Baba's grip, but he didn't let go. It didn't matter what *I* had decided, I couldn't break away when I wanted to because the big grip wouldn't allow me.

Frustrated, confused, aware of the crowd—physically still sitting at tables eating, but mentally gathered around us in a circle—Baba, being Baba, was forced to do something animal.

He took my smashed lunch and smacked the whole thing into my face. I was blinded as he twisted it, rubbing acidy orange pulp and mayonnaise into my eyes.

"How is it, is it good, rat?" Baba screamed as he jammed me. "You're so cool now, rat, you're so much *better* than me now. I really look up to your ass, Mick."

I was on my back and Baba was on my chest. This had happened before, of course, probably a thousand times over ten years. But this time, for the first time, I was terrified. I didn't know this creature on me, and it didn't know me. I was actually praying when three teachers and about twelve students pulled him off, the kids kicking and whinging and pulling hair. Not that I was popular enough to rate passionate help. It was just the rule, the opportunity rule. Helpers are allowed to take their shots, blind, anonymous rips at a guy from behind, as long as they do succeed in stopping the fight. They let you do that here. Baba knew the rule, took it in stride, didn't seem to care.

The thing that mattered to me, though, watching from flat on the floor, trying to rub clear my stinging eyes, was that the skinny guy with both arms wrapped around Baba's head like he was wrestling a medicine ball, was the acknowledged king of the cowards, Sullivan. Those same thousand times over those same ten years, Sully had stayed on the sidelines. Now when I needed it, when I didn't expect it, he was there.

The other thing that mattered was that I got jug.

I didn't even do anything to get it. I was committed to not getting it. Baba decides to sit on me, and I get it. It's like I'm shackled to the same old shit, stuck inside this useless school, stuck with idiot Baba because somewhere it says that I can't be allowed to shake any of it.

Sully too. Not that I didn't want him around some of the time, but there was a time and a place for him too. We weren't kids anymore, spending every minute of every day inside each other's shirt. I guess he missed me while I was out, because he followed me to detention after school. He was, in all likelihood, the first sap *ever* to want to get into the jug without being thrown in. And the monitor told him to scram. Pretty low, getting rejected by jug. He waited down on the sidewalk for me.

But Sully turned out to be about the only person who *wasn't* in jug. Baba was there, of course, big red-eyed steroid mountain sitting in the back, drinking milk out of a cardboard half-gallon, pus white running out of the corners of his mouth. Ruben was there, Evelyn's brother, his legs crossed, his feet resting on the desk across the aisle from him. I tried to give him a cool nod, figuring I should maybe start buddying up if I was going to be living with his sister. But in return he cracked open a book and stuck his nose in it—his version of "kiss my ass, junior."

The regulars were all there, the gum chewers, the destroyers of school property, the food spitters, the groin grabbers. Then, about ten minutes late, Toy made his slinking entrance. Hat pulled low, he shuffled across the front of the room, slapped his slip down on the desk, picked up his new slip for being late, and poured himself into the seat just in front of me.

I was excited to see him, even happy to be detained for it. "Yo, *compadre*," I said, shaking him by the shoulder.

He wriggled out of my grip, turned around slowly. "Com-*what*?" he growled.

"I said hey. It's good to see you."

He turned his back to me again. "So what? I saw you on Friday."

"Ya but, you know, I'm back. And you're back. We're back."

"Ya, you're back. So where are you back *from*, huh, Mick? Mars? Middle Earth?"

"Jesus, Toy, lighten up."

"I don't hang with losers. You want to screw yourself up, just go do it. I've got no time. I've got no patience."

I was getting nervous, like I was flunking something I really wanted to pass. Beer flashed through my mind, made my mouth water. I pushed it out. "I'm not a loser. I'm not like that."

He let me squirm for a minute. "You do smell better."

I smiled, relieved. I felt like a good boy. Though he didn't turn right around, he seemed to hear me relax.

"But, Mick," he said, finally showing me his face, or rather, his hat. "You know how many chances you get, to show me what you are?"

I shrugged. "How many?"

"I'll give you a hint. You already used it up."

A paper clip went zing off my ear, making it burn. I turned around to catch the guilty one. All of them, they were the guiltiest-looking bunch of people I ever saw in one classroom.

"Damn," I said, rubbing my ear. "I can't believe I'm here."

Toy said, casually, "You want to not be here?"

I gave him a face. "Course I don't want to be here."

He started getting up. "What are you doing?" I asked.

"I'm getting us released." He grinned. "I got a little leverage with the man."

I sat dumbstruck as Toy walked up, stood

towering over the monitor, who looked up with a weird embarrassment on his pointy bluish face. "I'm sick," Toy said, in a particularly healthy-sounding voice. He spoke just loud enough for the people up front—me and the monitor—to hear. "I have to go."

The monitor nodded.

Toy pointed at me. "He's sick too."

The monitor gestured quickly for me to get up and out, then buried himself in papers again. Walking across the front of the room, I felt a surge of power as I watched every jaw in the place drop to the floor. Ruben's eyes bugged. Baba's narrowed.

"Hey, can he come?" I said to Toy, indicating Ruben.

Toy knew what I was up to. "Points?" he asked, mockingly.

I tried to be indignant. "No, I'm not trying to score points with anyone. Maybe I just like the guy."

Toy actually snickered over that, as he walked back to the desk. "Ya, maybe you do," he said.

"Cruz, get outta here," the monitor snapped.

Ruben hopped out of his seat and made a grand exit, extra bounce in his step, big smiles, eye contact, and nods for everybody left behind.

On the way out the door I took one more look toward the back of the room, where Baba was taking good long note of the three of us together.

"Jeez, Toy," I said, "with that kind of power, why do you ever show up at jug at all?"

He refused to enjoy it, which drove me crazy. "You can't use something like that every day, or you lose it altogether."

"So, give it up," Ruben said. "Whatchu got on him?"

"Nothing," Toy answered in his now familiar end-of-discussion deep rasp. "You can go back in there if you want."

Ruben raised his hands, surrender-style. "I didn't ask no questions. I don't need to know nothing."

When we opened the front doors, Sully was there, waiting for me on the corner. When he saw Toy and Ruben, he hung his head and walked off. I called him once, but he didn't answer. I thought about chasing after him, but I couldn't do that. Sully was going to have to come around to new stuff. He had to. I wasn't going back, and he wasn't going to hold me back.

Toy, Ruben and I went to the superette, sat outside on milk crates, and smoked little cigars like we did before. I sat back and listened as Toy and Ruben talked about Cuban cigars, which I had never had, and how much better they were than Dominican ones. They talked about some other stuff I didn't know too, talked some of it in Spanish. I felt kind of foreign, and I felt kind of lost, but I figured it would pass.

El Micko

We slipped back into the old routine of meeting at the superette before and after school to smoke cigars. We hadn't even discussed it, just found each other there at the right times again. Except this time there was no Sully, there was Ruben. He could have come, Sully, if he wanted to. The thing is he just doesn't like new people, doesn't like things to change, can't deal with new stuff. Me, I needed new stuff.

My first new thing, besides Evelyn I guess, and besides Ruben, who was such new stuff he was frightening, was I got a hat. I went down to Walker's, the one place in town that has all the hardest-core biker gear and all the real cowboy gear, which up close turns out to be pretty much the same thing. I looked the walls up then down, at high black square-toed mechanic boots, pointy gray snakeskin Acme cowboy boots, green lizard Tony Lamas, Dingos, spurs for jabbing your horse or motorcycle into going faster, T-shirts with big old Harley-Davidson eagles spread across the back and wolves or buffalo or mountain lions or black bears snarling on the front. There was a pair of size 14 elephant-skin boots. I felt like a better man just being there.

If I had the money I would have walked out of Walker's taller than I was, wearing those black, knee-high square-toed mothers with the stainless steel tips. But I didn't have the money for that yet so I bought the hat. The scoop-top Georgia straw hat with the brim bent all the way low to my nose in front and practically to the top of my shirt collar in back. I had to tilt my head back to see how I looked in the mirror, but that was fine because what I saw there looked *cool*, cooler ten thousand times than anything I'd ever seen there before, and the tilt of the head only made it look cooler.

And it did make me taller too. I knew I'd shopped well when I went to leave the house with it on in the morning and Terry yelled from the table, "Yo, Buckeroo Buttlick, take that stupid-ass wastebasket off your head before you go out-side and embarrass the whole family."

"Shut up, Terry," Dad said in a dumb big whisper that I wasn't supposed to hear but of course I did. "If you don't talk about the damn stupid thing, he'll take it off in a couple a days."

I didn't answer them, because that was becoming one of my favorite things to do, not answering them. I marched out, slammed the door, and bounded down the stairs, knowing how much slicker, and taller, I was now.

Until I saw Toy. As he watched me come up on the superette, he got up off his crate. I felt a big not-quite-cool grin open up my face but it was okay because the hat had it mostly covered. When I stood in front of him, I was ready to burst waiting for his comment.

He slapped it right off my head.

I stood, no longer smiling as I watched Toy kick the hat into the gutter. Water actually welled up in my eyes, even though there was no reason for it, none. He didn't slap *me*, he wouldn't do that, but he slapped the hell out of that hat. And I sort of expected a lot out of that hat. Expected a lot out of me *in* it. Expected a lot out of Toy.

"You're not me," he said, stomping the hat. It

half sounded as if he was addressing the hat, not me. "Don't *try* to be me, don't *pretend* to be me, don't *aspire* to be me."

I had seen Toy be intense before, and even inexplicably strange. I hadn't seen him be nuts before, though. His voice didn't go up higher than usual, he didn't rant, just stomp stomp stomped my new Georgia straw bent brim hat from Walker's. I didn't quite know whether to be more hurt or more afraid of him. I knew which way I *felt*, though. I turned to walk on to school.

"Wait a minute," he said.

I waited, as he slowly picked the beat-up hat off the ground and walked toward me. "I'm sorry," he said.

But he didn't give it back.

He continued on to the trash barrel, dumped the hat inside. Then he came back to me, stuck a ten-dollar bill in my hand. The hat cost me twenty-five. And it would cost me a lot more if Terry ever got around to counting the gym bag full of one-dollar bills in the corner of his closet and found out I stole a fistful.

"That should cover it," Toy said. "I mean, I hope you didn't pay more than that for that piece of crap."

I stuck the ten in my pocket. "No, come on, what do you think, I'm stupid?"

"I'm sorry," he repeated. He didn't add anything like an explanation, but he'd already said sorry twice more than I would have expected. He stuck an obscenely fat cigar in my hand and sat back down on his milk crate. "Cuban," he said as he lit one for himself.

"Here, this is better for you anyway," Ruben said, popping up and jamming his own hat on my head from behind.

I spun to look at him.

"*Bueno,*" he said, nodding several times and smiling his broad, no-front-teeth smile. "Wanna know what I think, you looked pretty stupid in that cowboy hat anyway."

"You were watching," I said, feeling a new level of stupid.

"Right over there," he said, pointing to a mailbox across the street. "Thing is, Mike—"

"Mick."

"Thing is, you gotta be a big *persona* to gedawaywit wearing something like that." He pointed at Toy with his thumb. "This one, big. Beeeeeg *persona*. And you know what? Even he can't gedawaywidit. Look like a big dope, don't he?" Cruz laughed and walked up to Toy, who stuck out his hand. "*¿Porqué,* man? Acting all mental already, so early in the morning. Beating up on the guy's *sombrero*?"

They shook hard and Toy blew smoke in Ruben's face, squeezing his hand harder and harder until Ruben's knees bent. He didn't make a sound, though, or ask Toy to stop.

I took the hat off and checked it out. It was like an old man's hat, a gray felt fedora with a black band. Inside was a bright yellow silk lining. The hat Ruben always wore. I fixed it back on my head.

"It fits you nice," he said, walking up to me to adjust it to about a forty-five degree backward tilt. "There you go. You know, you're taller than me, but I do have this really big head. Everybody says so." He bent down to give me the full on-top view of his head.

"I see," I said.

"It's good on you, Mick," Toy said easily, like nothing had happened.

"It feels good," I said, sliding it off then on again.

Ruben turned to Toy again. "If you're happy, I'm happy." Then to me. "If you're happy, I'm happy. The hat is yours." He held out his hand. "Ten dollars."

"You were watching pretty close," I said, pulling out the ten Toy'd just handed me.

"All *right*," Ruben laughed. "Now I can go out and buy me ten more a them cheap-ass hats."

To close the deal, Ruben pulled out his lighter and lit my cigar. Toy threw one to Ruben and soon we were all floating in a fog of Havana smoke.

"*Dios mío*, this is freakin' fan*ta*stic," Ruben said, and they both nodded. They made moans and yumm sounds like they were munching chocolate-covered macadamia nuts. The first long pull tasted strong, bitter, but good, burning up inside my sinuses. Then I started going downhill. My stomach jumped, I got a headache, and the back of my mouth started watering uncontrollably, prevomit condition.

"It's almost time for school," I warbled as I stubbed out the ash on the sidewalk. "I'm gonna save this for later."

I didn't wait for any response. The two of them looked knowingly at each other, and I just started walking, weaving like a drunk toward the school, trying to hold it together. The street ahead floated in a heat-vapor wave, making me sicker. In a few seconds, they were there again, Toy on my left side, Ruben on my right, bumping me with their shoulders, keeping me up and steady. They knew. But they didn't make me say it.

By the time we reached the school, I was clearer. Not quite lifelike yet, but better. I still needed a minute of air before going into the school, which always smelled like wet smoke and oil paint anyway. Toy was going inside. He stopped to look me over again.

"You look good," he said, pointing at the hat, or maybe at my face. I reached up to rub my hot-then-cold temple, and the skin felt like the skin on old pudding left in the back of the refrigerator.

"I do?" I asked.

"You do. *Cambio está bueno,*" he said as he went in. "I'll catch you later."

Ruben was still next to me. "What did he say?" I asked him.

"He said you was a asshole."

"Thanks," I said.

"Hey, you know, you done all right," Ruben said. "Smokin' on that big ol' Cubano. You didn't fall down or nothin', so that was pretty good."

"Thanks again," I said. "Listening to you is gonna give me a big head, the way you throw around compliments."

"Serious, Mark—"

"Mick."

"Serious, that was a little kindova test, and you passed it all right. You might not turn out ta be such a stupid shit as you seem."

I didn't suppose it was going to get any better than this, so I made my little pitch.

"Listen, Ruben, man, I know we didn't always

get along too good, but I think we should put all that stuff in the past. All right with you?"

"All right with me. Long's you don't turn out ta be no fool. You got a rep, man. As a big-time fool."

"Ya, well, that rep's wrong."

"No it ain't. I seen you be a fool. I seen you on TV. And if there's anybody stupider than a ordinary fool, it's somebody who be's a fool on the TV."

The goddamn sonofabitch TV thing. Did I think that it went away? Did I think people forgot? Did I think that somehow, the day Baba cleaned my clock that he somehow cleaned everybody's, wiping out all the time that came before then? Yes. I did think that. But every time I heard it mentioned again, I wished Baba or somebody could please come and hit me in the head again, and again, and again, so I wouldn't have to hear it even once more.

"Okay, man, the rep wasn't wrong, exactly, but it's out of date. I'm not that. Not now."

The bell screeched, calling us inside.

"Okay," Ruben said, shrugging, walking in.

That was easy, I thought. So I swung for the fences. "You know, I'm kind of seeing your sister, so we might be seeing—"

"*My* sister?" he asked, appearing shocked.

"Ya, Evelyn. So—"

"I ain't got no sister Evelyn. I got a sister Juana."

"Juana?"

"And listen, if you gonna wear the hat, you gotta button your shirt." He stepped up and buttoned my shirt tight at the neck. Then he yanked the shirttail out of my pants. I looked like I was in the band Los Lobos. "Gotta let it *hang*, baby," he said, stepping back to admire me. "Pants are too tight, and the shoes are all wrong, but you's movin' the right way."

"Okay, but about me and your sister—"

"Forget it. My sista's too ol' for you. She don't live around here anyway. Find somebody your own . . . style."

"I don't want . . ." I said, but he ducked into a classroom as the bell rang. He had me confused, thinking more about Evelyn, wanting to talk to her. But I started toward class, and as I felt myself move, felt the collar grabbing at my neck, the hat sitting up there, the shirt *hangin'*, I lightened up. I swung when I walked. I felt a little different. Which is to say I felt good.

Sully stared me naked as I walked down to the seat right in front of him. "What the hell happened to you?"

"I don't know what you're talking about," I

said, turning my back to him.

"Yes you do," he said. "You're all greased up. Like the spaniels. You a spaniel now, Mick?"

I turned around in my seat. "Y'know, Sul, you're a real ignoramus when you want to be."

"Hey, I may be an ignoramus, but at least I ain't no pretend spaniel just to get a little face off some chick."

Even as he said it he looked like he was afraid, and he should have been. But he looked more angry, at me, for whatever.

"Hey, Sul, remember when we were ten and you whipped that kid with the car antenna 'cause he was kickin' my ass? Well, because you did that, I'm not killin' you now. But remember, you only saved me that one time."

He gave me the cold fish eye. "So, what about next week, you gonna be an Indian with the war paint and feathers hanging down to yer ass?"

I didn't hit him. He knew I wouldn't, which was why he could say stuff like that. But I didn't talk to him either. I folded my hands like I always do when I'm sitting at a desk and I don't know what else to do. In a minute, he spoke. He had no heart for the cold shoulder, just like he was too soft for most things.

"Anyway," he said in the same middle-of-nowhere voice that he says everything, "Honey's

77

gonna meet us after school. She's gonna be outside. So tuck in your shirt and take that damn
stupid greasy thing off your head."

This is why I had to start sort of ignoring
Sully. I couldn't tell anymore if he was deaf, or
insane, or just completely stupid. I used to be
able to tell. Used to be able to tell everything
about him, more than he could himself. When
we were six, eight, fourteen years old. Not so now
though. It was like at this point he didn't understand a thing I said. Like that I wanted no parts
of his sister. So I was just going to have to leave
him alone for a while. He'd get better again.

I went the whole day without earning detention,
and when the last bell rang I raced downstairs to
wait at the door for Evelyn. In my new style. I
couldn't lose.

I stood in the middle of the sidewalk at the
foot of the school steps, so that the road out led
to me. I could *feel* my look again, and it made me
bold. I spread my feet wide, clasped my hands
behind my back and waited. As students filed
out, I sorted, mentally plucking and tossing aside
every one who was not Evelyn.

Then, one of them was Toy.

"Sunglasses," he said, walking right up to me
and blocking my view. "You need some sun-

glasses to complete the look. Wayfarers, maybe."

"It's not even sunny. It looks like it's gonna rain, even."

He clicked his tongue at me, the way parents do. "You still need a lot of work, boy."

"I know, but can we work later?" I said, and pushed Toy out of my way. Pushed? Yes I did, I pushed Toy. When I realized what I'd done, I looked up at him with the right amount of fear and regret.

Fortunately, what he dropped on me was a fatherly smile. "This must be love," he said, backing up to sit on the steps. "It's got to be love. It *better* be love." He pointed a big finger at me then, but it sounded like he was more happy about it than mad.

I waited, watching for her again.

Ruben came bounding down the stairs. *"¡Amigo!"* he said, rushing up to me. I heard Toy laughing in the background. "You waitin' for me? How sweet."

I looked beyond him, over his head for his sister. Where was she? "Don't you have some other friends to play with for now?" I said. Not that I could really afford to be risking any myself.

He was offended. "If I did, would I be hangin' wit*chu*?"

"Mira," Toy called, motioning Ruben to him.

"I'll tell you all about it." They sat together, watching me, muttering and laughing. My new cool was quickly running out all over the sidewalk.

All the other people I didn't want to see passed, a lot of them checking me out and smirking. Baba thumped by, brushing me with his shoulder and tossing me a look that was like spit.

Finally, finally, Evelyn emerged. A few strides behind her, a rotten freak of luck but the kind of luck I'm overblessed with, was Sully.

Evelyn's eyes widened, and I remembered my look. I straightened, spread the feet again, clasped the hands at the back again.

"¿El Micko?" she said, then politely covered her mouth as she began to laugh at me again.

"I'm going the hell home," I said, to the background hum of Toy's, Ruben's, and Sully's chuckles. It was only then she knew they were all there. She grabbed me by the hand, yanked me close to her.

"Please, it was laughter of admiration, I promise."

Whatever the hell laughter of admiration is. But the words didn't matter at all. What did matter was that her nose was pressed against the tip of my ear when she said it. Everything else washed away. Ruben for one and Sully for two didn't seem to like that, at all. Toy mimed a little golf clap of approval.

"Let's go someplace," I said. "Want to?"

"Sure," she said.

I was nearly trotting, trying to get out of there. Evelyn pulled me back by the shirt. "Easy. Where you running to?"

"No place," I said. I saw that a few steps behind was Sully, following us. A few steps behind him were Ruben and Toy. "What you should have asked was what am I running *from*?" I said, pointing at the group.

Evelyn turned. "Well, hello, boys. Mick, this is very impressive. You have an entourage. Are you a boxer? A president?"

"I'm a fugitive," I said, grabbing her hand and hurrying on. We had just started putting a little distance between us and them when we were stopped dead again. In front of the superette.

"Yes, hello, Honey," I said, like the air running out of a balloon. "Nice to see you too."

"Honey?" Evelyn said to me with arched brows. "Friend of yours?"

"That's her name. Honey, this is Evelyn. Evelyn, Honey."

While they shook hands and said their nice-to-meet-you's, Sully caught up. "He did have an appointment, you know," he said, taking his place beside Honey, looking at Evelyn as he talked.

"He did?" Evelyn looked at me.

"No. Sully, cut the shit."

"He was meeting my sister here," Sully said, again to Evelyn.

Toy and Ruben caught up, took their seats on the milk crates, and lit up.

"Hey, I could leave," Evelyn said. "I've got things to do anyway."

I *would* kill him over this. "Sul, man, I don't know what you're trying to achieve here, but I'll kick your balls through the top of your head if you don't—"

"Oh *that's* pretty," Evelyn said, drawing from Sully a small victorious smile. He was getting me to do his work for him.

"Sorry," I said. "I'm really not like that. I don't know what—"

"Listen," Honey cut in. "We didn't have no date or nothin' special like that. I was just comin' out ta meet the boys is all. Don't let me get in the way. You two make a nice-lookin' pair."

Sully turned tomato red. "Whatsa matter with you? You wanna be a old friggin' maid or what?"

Toy and Ruben started commenting from

within their cloud. "Booo!" they called at Sully. "Booooo! Go home. You stink."

He was about to say more, not to them, but to Honey, when Evelyn headed him off. "That's such a pretty name you have." She hummed it, "Honey . . . Honey. It must be beautiful to hear it all day."

Honey looked down, then up at Evelyn, smiling a shy smile. She looked unsure whether to believe the compliment or not. She probably wasn't used to it. Honey was what the local ladies referred to as "plain" when they were pretending to be kind. Plain. Stop-a-train plain. But she seemed to live with that okay and never turned nasty over it the way some people would. Just stayed, like her name, sweet all the time. What she did have, though, was a pretty unbelievable body, the whole tight, hourglass, nothing missing package, settled under that big unfortunate head. That sorry kind of girl who, you know, all the guys want to take *on*, but none of them want to take *out*. Which, I hear, is what happens to her a lot.

"But it's not really my real name," she said. "My real name is Esther. A teacher started calling me Honey when I was younger, because, he said, I was such a sweet thing, and it stuck. That's a nice thing, don't you think?"

I watched Evelyn smile, reach out, and touch Honey's hand as gently as you'd stroke a new kitten. "That's a very nice thing," she said.

"But Evelyn is a pretty name too, of course," Honey said.

Evelyn backed away from that. "Yes," she mumbled. Ruben hooted at her.

"Ya, about *your* name . . ." I said. "Is your name really Juana?"

She threw her brother a wicked stare. He looked at his feet.

"You can call me Evelyn," she said harshly to me. "Or you can not call me at all."

"Evelyn, Evelyn, Evelyn, Evelyn . . ." I said.

Even Toy seemed amused now. "Juaaana," he said, drawn out and exaggerated. "Hhhhwwwaaaa-nnnaaa."

She marched right up to him. "Yes? *Angel?* What can I do for you, Anhelll?"

"Hey," he snapped, but she didn't move.

"You have the most beautiful name of all, and you hide it. What's that all about?"

"I like Toy," he said, retreating.

"I like Angel," she said.

"I like Angel too," I said.

"I like *Toy*," he barked at me.

"You're right," I said. "Toy sounds better."

Ruben pointed at me. "This is freakin' fun. Yo, Matt, what's your real name?"

"Mick," I said. I'd rather have said Esther.

"No, isn't it really Michael?" Evelyn said because she knows everything.

The muck of my embarrassment was up over my ankles now, heading for my knees. "No, it's actually Mick. My father thought Mick was the coolest thing, for reasons of his own, and I'd rather not go into it any further."

Luckily, nobody else wanted to go into it any further, either. With the silence, Sully found his moment to get back into it.

"So, you gonna take my sister out, or what?" he said, deadly serious.

I had to smile. "I'm sorry, Honey," I said.

"For what? Don't worry about it. I got plenty a boyfriends."

"No, Sul. I'm not gonna take Honey out."

"I will," Ruben said, jumping up and scurrying to her. He stood smiling up—she was a head taller than him—wiggling his tongue in the spaces where his teeth weren't. She smiled back.

"The hell you *will*," Sully said, grabbing her by the arm and whisking her away.

"Nice meeting you all," Honey called back.

"Bunch a friggin' phonies," Sully called.

Evelyn walked to me. "We were going some-place?" she asked.

"We were."

As we started to walk away, Ruben hopped up behind us again. "I'm havin' a great freakin' time today. Where we goin' now?"

"Come on, man," I said. Begged, actually. "Give us a break. Go hang with some of your other friends for a while."

"He hasn't *got* any," Evelyn snapped.

"I do so got friends. I got two. But they dead now."

Toy stepped up behind him, grabbed Ruben by the collar. "Have a good time," he said, waving to us.

"I want to apologize, for Sully," I said when I finally knew what I wanted to say. "He's just crude. He's ignorant and, I don't know, I feel like he's something I should apologize for."

We were walking up the stairs of the old brick boathouse by the pond, to watch the boats and the ducks and the still water.

"Don't apologize," she said. "You should be proud. That boy loves you a lot."

Augie's Dogs

etting out of my neighborhood, or
getting out of my *family*, was a lot like
getting out of the priesthood. You
couldn't just wake up one day and say "Okay,
I'm not what I was anymore," and that would
be it. There was a lot of explaining to do,
maybe some vows to be broken.

Also, both groups were big on ceremonies,
and holidays. The big one in the neighborhood
was of course St. Pat's. But that one was a lot of
show, and open to the public. The event that
probably said more about The Terry Style was
May Day. Because it was more secret. Because it
was more violent. And because it neatly summed

up my brother's worldview: If you aren't in our circle, then you're in our sights.

Could it be May Day again already? Seemed like it was only last week it was May Day and all of us were sitting on the Cambridge side of the river at three A.M. watching the bonfire. Terry had broken into the boat shed and dragged out all the equipment of not one but two college crew clubs to make his personal flaming tribute to higher education. No actual boats—though he tried his ass off to get one out—but life jackets, rubber shoes, oars, white plastic first-aid boxes, and a generous splash of 151 rum that made a foul, brilliant, chemical-fueled green and blue and yellow and red flame that reflected off the flat river and popped with small explosions.

If I was at all serious about making a break from all the ignorance once and for all, I had to break from May Day. Only it's not just a day. It's forty-eight fearsome hours over the second weekend in May when Terry and his disciples gather and celebrate the exodus from *their* town of all the "faggot-ass college students who don't belong here anyhow." It officially starts on Saturday morning when Augie blows in through the front door towing two cases of Ballantine ale and his two dogs, Bunky and Bobo. He plunks himself down in front of the TV, turns up World

Wide Main Event Super Heavyweight Battle of the Ages Championship Wrestling so loud you can hear the fighters drool, and he cracks open his first bottle.

From my bedroom I heard the first "psshht."

"Did I hear a beer?" Terry yelled as he threw open his bedroom door. He punched my door loud on the way by.

"Have fun, you boys," Ma said as she hurried to scram. My parents do their part by making their one smart move of the year. They clear out. Last year it was to Franconia to visit their friend the rich ignorant plumbing contractor who eats with his mouth wide open. This year it was North Conway for knickknack crap nobody wants.

"Don't break nothin' this year, Augie," Dad growled just before stomping out. "And if you do, replace it before I get back."

I heard Augie laugh. "Lighten up, old guy. Here ya go, have a suck for the road."

There was a pause. "It's a two-hour ride, for chrissake," Dad said, disgusted.

"Pardon me," Augie said, then I heard a lot of clinking as Dad left with an armful of bottles.

For a half hour the two of them yelled at the TV, belched, crashed around the living room body-slamming each other, hurled empty bottles down the hall, and howled high-pitched howls to make the dogs crazy so that together they sounded like a four-mutt barbershop quartet. I stayed in bed with my pillow over my head. Jesus, I hope they forget about me, I thought.

"Hey! Get yer ass out here . . . you," Terry screamed from the bathroom as he took a loud leak with the door open. "You're way behind. You don't wanna miss the May Day festivities."

Oh yes I did. I was there last year and the year before and the year before, back to when I reached the local official drinking age of twelve. I liked it then, drunk off my ass and puking up more guts than I ever thought I had just because Southern Comfort tasted a little too much like berries. And I didn't even mind it too much last year when I got clocked by that big stupid college rent-a-cop, because, well, I did hit him first and I was holding the spray paint can and I did after all get the big laughs I was after when I painted him to begin with.

But not now. As I listened to Terry and Augie and Bunky and Bobo yuck it up just a few feet away doing what they'd done before, only now they sounded like I didn't even know them even though I knew them too damn well, I had but one thought. And that was to run. This was not a good place for me, and it would get worse quickly.

I needed a shower. I didn't take one. I pulled on yesterday's dirty baggies, buttoned my shirt up to my neck, watched my hands shake as I pulled on my socks and shoes. I threw on my Ruben Cruz fedora and stepped lively out toward the front door.

"Hey," Terry ordered. "Get your sneaky little ass down here."

I stood with my hand on the knob, thinking about just going.

"Don't *make* us send Bobo after you," Augie laughed.

Bobo is a shiny brown, square, mean and stupid Rottweiler–Great Dane mix, almost as tall as me. He looks like a UPS truck, and is legend for throwing himself on whatever Augie tells him to, even a moving police car once.

I turned and walked back to the living room.

"Where are you goin'?" Terry asked. "Din' you hear me jus' tell you it was May Day?"

"Yo, Mickey-boy," Augie said from way down in my father's soft, shredded armchair, "you wanna see what Bobo can do?"

"No."

Terry bellowed. "No? No, you didn't hear me tell you it was May Day? What are you, goddamn deaf or goddamn stupid? Augie, you hear me tell him, like, pretty goddamn loud?"

91

"Heard ya, bro. Personally, I think he's god-damn stupid, not goddamn deaf."

"No. I didn't say no I didn't hear you, Terry. I said no I didn't want to see Bobo's stupid trick."

"Here, watch," Augie said anyway. He reached over to the end table beside him, took a bottle cap and dunked it into a bowl of onion dip, covering two fingers and a thumb up to the knuckle. "Bo. Yo, Bo," he said, and flipped the dog the coated metal cap. Bobo snapped it out of the air and chewed on it, crunching and grinding until he'd pulverized it, then swallowing. When he finished, he scooted up closer and sat in begging position in front of Augie. Augie tossed him another cap, without dip, and the dog did the same thing again.

By now, Terry had walked right up to me. He smelled bitter like vomit even though it was still a little early for that. "So like I said, where are ya goin'?"

"I'm going out," I said.

It was as if he had prepared this, had been waiting for it. "Ya ain't supposed ta be goin' nowhere, ya supposed ta be wid us. Ya wid us, Mick?" He spoke low, which was not his way, and with a smile, which was not his way. Slowly, he reached up and unbuttoned the top button of my shirt. "We don't do that," he said. "Ya made a mistake, when you was dressin' so fast."

Then he reached down and started tucking the front of my shirt into my pants, never taking his eyes from my eyes. "Yer just such a mess taday, boyo. Ya don't know which end is up, do ya?"

I didn't look away either. I stared right into him as I slowly raised my hands and started buttoning my top button again. "I like it this way. No mistake."

"*Mistake*," he snarled, and as he tucked, jammed his fist down into my pants. I froze.

"Now ya wanna see what Bunky can do?" Augie chirped. "It's even better, 'cause he's a lot smarter than Bobo. He's the brains, Bobo's the brawn."

"Get it out," I said to Terry.

"In a minute I will. When I'm ready." He reached up with his free hand and snatched the hat off my head. With his knuckles still jammed against my balls, he tossed the hat into the middle of the floor. "Get it, Bobo," he said, and when after a few seconds Augie repeated the order, Bobo set himself on the hat. He pressed it to the floor with his big paws and with his mouth tore at the felt like it was wet paper. First he made about a dozen jerky strips, then swallowed each one.

Terry yanked his hand out of my pants, stepping back and smirking. "I had ya. I let ya go. I can have ya again, anytime I want. Remember."

I gave him no reaction, except to untuck my shirt again.

"So, pull up ya chair, boy," Augie said, uncapping a Ballantine short-neck bottle and aiming it at me.

"No," I said.

"Why no?" Augie was genuinely puzzled.

"Because I don't want it," I said.

He stared at me, head tilted to one side. "Your hair's gettin' pretty damn long there, kid."

"I know it is." I was starting to feel it, starting to feel the closing in all around. I started to sweat.

"I ain't seen him take so much as a sip lately, Augie," Terry said, snatching the bottle from him. He brought it to me, stuck it under my nose. "Lost the taste, have ya, Mick?"

It was then I realized that I hadn't. The carbon bubbles were popping, tickling, carrying the strong yeasty Ballantine head up into my nostrils. My mouth watered, but my stomach clenched.

"You need a haircut, freak," Augie said.

I pushed the bottle away from my face. "You're right," I said, pointing at Augie. "I do.

And I'm gonna get one, right now." I quickly started backing way, back toward the front door.

"So have a goddamn blast before ya go," Terry said, following me halfway to the door with the bottle. "Get back here and drink the damn thing." His voice rose. "It ain't like the goddamn barber shop is goin' any goddamn place."

"I don't *want* it," I said.

He was infuriated now. He ran to catch me at the door, but I ran faster to get away. He screamed at me from the porch. "What are you, *good*? You *good* now or somethin', Mick?" And he heaved the full bottle at me, missing me by a mile as it shattered and splattered on the curb.

Sully loves me. What is she talking about, Sully loves me? What a mental thing to say. A lot that'll get me anyhow, Sully's love. That'll get me far.

Whether I believed it or not, that's where I found myself when I escaped, Sully's house. I stood there on the sidewalk looking up at his bedroom window, in the house that looked just like my house. Like I'd done a hundred thousand times before when I was just looking for some-place to go to that wasn't my place, that didn't have my parents or my brother inside. The differ-ence though was that this time I didn't have two fingers in my mouth whistling myself blue for him to come down and claim me. This time I looked, stared up there like a freak on the sidewalk, and went on my way. If he had just happened to come to the window that would have been okay, I could maybe have stayed there for the weekend till May Day blew over, if he invited me. But he didn't, and I couldn't call or whistle for him this time. It just didn't feel like I could do that now.

I walked on, no destination, just on. I thought about it, where I wasn't going, and felt a small scared shiver. It was the same nothing for me in both directions, forward and back. I had no home. My parents had cleared out, surrendered the place to the barbarians. Never even mentioned it to me, that they wouldn't be around for a couple of days. And even though this was a regular thing for May Day and even though we all know they are going, is that right, that they shouldn't say something to me? It's like, the *home*, it isn't *there* for me.

But it was never important before, so it wasn't important now. There were other places for me, even if they were few.

"Hey freakin' ho, *muchacho*, ain't this a damn treat," Ruben said as he pulled back the curtain from the small front door window. I listened as he unlocked three dead bolts, then threw the door wide open. "This may surprise you, but I don't get a whole lotta visitors, specially on no Saturday morning."

It was such a happy, welcoming thing, Ruben's broad gap-toothed smile, that it almost made me feel right. It almost made nothing else matter. "You want some breakfast?" he said. "I think I got a egg and a little skinny-ass frozen sausage."

But I had to tell him the truth. "Thanks, man, that's really nice. But actually, I'm here to see Evelyn. Is she home?"

Slam. Bolt, bolt, bolt. Ruben was gone from view and the door was again well secured. I sighed, rang the bell again.

"Who is it?" Ruben's voice sang from the other side of the door.

"Come on, Cruz, it's me."

His small fine face appeared in the window again. "Jehovah's Witness?" he asked.

"No. I'm here to see Evelyn."

"Evelyn?"

"Your sister. Cut the shit."

"Sorry, I ain't got no sister Evelyn. You mean Juana?"

"Fine. I mean Juana."

"I ain't got no sister Juana. Listen you, you

better get outta here or I'm gonna put the dog on you. I mean it."

I turned and walked down the stairs as Ruben went into an inspired fit of snarling and yowling and hurling himself against the door. I hopped the fence, passed the Mary and flamingo statues, and snuck around to the back door, hoping Evelyn could possibly hear the knock before her brother White Fang cut it off. But just as I turned the corner in back, I was blasted backward by a growl so low and nasty I didn't hear it, I felt it under my feet.

A dog. They had a dog, a real dog, a massive black dog on a chain with a spiked collar, a dog too mean even to bark for fear that victims wouldn't get close enough for mangling. He curled one lip at me as he growled, a red pulpy piece of something hanging off a lower front tooth while the rest of the pulpy red something—maybe it was a rabbit or a cat or a smaller dog—lay a few feet away at the entrance to its tar-papered dog shed.

I backed out of the yard, watching the beast, my whole body shaking.

"Whatchu think, I be *lyin'* 'bout my dog?" Cruz laughed from the porch as I passed. "I don't know what you was thinkin' that you could jus' come on over here an' y'know, have your way an' shit . . ."

I walked away as quickly as I could, with my legs still rubbery from the dog scare. I didn't even look at Ruben.

"Hey, where you goin'? I thought we was gonna do somethin'?"

I didn't answer.

"Hey, I'm *talkin'* to you!" he yelled, trying to sound tough. In the next breath, though, he sounded like a little boy. "Where's the hat I gave you. . . ? Hey . . . I was just playin' . . ."

I couldn't play. Maybe later I could play but not now. I had, had, I *had* to have someplace I could go. I wasn't sure if there was such a place for me, but I did know there was a place that took in everybody.

I didn't feel so foreign this time, as I cruised the skanky streets on the east side of the school, past the neighborhoods that belonged to somebody else, down down deeper toward the bay, to that mongrel patchwork of a subcity for nowhere people. I felt kind of right when I got down to the fish-packing plants and slanty apartment houses of Toy's world.

"Is he here?" I asked hopefully, tentatively, though I somehow already knew that he wasn't.

"What are you talking about?" Felina asked wearily, sagging against the door frame. "It's the weekend. He isn't here on the weekend. This is the ghost house once Friday comes."

"I'm sorry . . ." I said, already wishing I hadn't come.

Everything was making me weak, draining me of life. Terry and Augie and Bunky and Bobo and Ballantine at nine. Sully-who-loves-me's house. Ruben's nightmare dog. Felina and her tired voice and her big black hollow eyes. I felt as sapped as Felina looked.

"Do you like coffee?" she asked, like the recorded time and temperature voice on the phone.

"I like coffee."

"Would you like some, coffee?"

"I would like some. Coffee."

I went in there, and up, up the stairs behind Felina. Into the house at the end of the world. I followed her, like I figured I was supposed to, not talking, as we passed through the living room where I met her that first time. But I didn't want to think about that. I followed her down a hallway so narrow that the knuckles of both of my hands brushed the walls as I walked. With a three-foot lead, Felina reached into doorways and yanked each door shut, two on the right, one on the left, before I could see in. "Wasn't expecting company," she said. "You understand."

In the kitchen, she pointed to a chair. I sat in it, an orange vinyl-covered swiveler on big ball casters. Three more like it surrounded the circular brown Formica table. The room felt small, maybe because of the grapefruit-size roses on the grease-bubbled wallpaper that seemed to be closing in from every direction.

"So," she said, stirring coffee in a saucepan on the stove top. "Why are you here?"

I hadn't expected that. What had I expected?

"Toy, right?" I said weakly. "I'm lookin' for Toy, remember?"

"Oh," she said, and kept on stirring. "It's just that, you weren't here last Saturday. Or the Saturday before. Or any of the other Saturdays. And the only other time I ever saw you, you seemed a little banged up and freaky."

I thought of three different things to say, none of which really answered her. "Should I go?" is what finally came out.

"Oh, but there was that other time," she said, walking toward me with the hot pan in her hand. She smiled shyly, slyly. "You did come here that one other time, didn't you?"

I swiveled side to side to side to side in my chair. Couldn't get that image out of my head now, of the first time I saw her, on the couch with her big old hairy husband and that other woman. Couldn't get the image out. She'd planted it back in my head just like that and I couldn't get it to stop playing over and over again. Didn't totally want to get it out, to tell the truth. Her back. Her long, smooth, S-curved red-brown back. If she wasn't here, in front of me, I could love that. But it was making me squirm now.

She pulled down two mismatched mugs from a tree in the middle of the table, held the pan high, and poured. She didn't comment on my long squiggly silence. Then she let me off the line. "But anyway, most of the time, is my point, most of the time you seem to show here when you're sort of limping. You limping now?"

"No," I said indignantly. I straightened up, stopped fidgeting in my seat, and grabbed my mug.

Felina picked up her mug too, took a sip. She winced, held the sip in her mouth, ran and spat it in the sink. "Don't drink that," she said, coming back to swipe my cup away. "I'm sorry. That was old stuff. I'm sorry. I have something else. I have these little packets, instant, but flavored, you know, vanilla, mocha. Came in the Sunday paper. I'm sorry."

It seemed like some really big thing to her, that she gave me bad coffee. Like she was in trouble now or something. She hurried to put on the kettle and tear open the foil pouches of instant coffee.

"It's not a big deal," I said. "I don't usually even have coffee. Probably I would have liked it just fine."

"You're a good boy," she said.

When finally she sat at the table across from me, I got a chance to study her face. It wasn't an old face. It had a lot of deep lines in it, and the skin around her eyes was a little gray, but still, it wasn't an old face. It wasn't, to me, a mother face.

"I don't think I'll buy this coffee," she said, sniffing and stirring. "It's weak." Then she looked up, looked at me looking at her. "Thirty-three," she said.

"What?" I got nervous and started looking down into my own cup. "Nah, I think it's fine. I'd buy it. Though I don't really know much—"

"I'm thirty-three."

"I didn't ask."

"No, but you're looking. And you're thinking. So there it is for you. I'm thirty-three, Angel is seventeen. You want me to do the math for you?"

I shook my head and sipped my coffee.

Felina pushed her coffee away with a frown, then waited. She was waiting for me to say something but nothing was coming to me. Except that vision of her on the couch again, but I didn't want to talk about *that*.

"I forget, did you ever tell me why you are here?" she asked, folding her arms.

"Ya, I was here for Toy, but he's not here so I should go. I have to get a haircut, I just remembered." And I was happy to remember, because I was getting nervous as a cat, though I didn't know why. I gulped down the coffee and started bowing and stumblebumming out of the room. "Thanks. Thank you. Tell Toy—"

"I could cut your hair."

Thrilled and scared at the same time, it came out like this: "Hummina hummina huh?"

She smiled a big wide, bright-white toothy smile. "I never cut a red before. I used to work in a salon. I'd love it, and save you a buck."

"Oh, there, ya see," I fumbled. "That wouldn't work for me. I don't do salons, I go to a barber."

She laughed, took me firmly by the hand. "I can barber."

I let her lead me like a balloon on a string. First, to the kitchen sink. "Hope you don't mind, but your hair is, well, filthy."

"I know," I said. "I had to leave kinda quickly this morning."

She sat me in a tall chair in front of the sink, gently tipped me back until my head was in the basin, my neck leaning on the edge. She sprayed me down with warm water, using one of those old gunlike rinsing hoses. As she worked the papaya shampoo into my head, my eyes fell closed and I relaxed.

"So what was the rush to get out of the house?" she asked.

"Sometimes, I just really, *really* can't stand to be home," I said.

"Hmmm. Carlo feels the same way. A *lot*. So does my son, as you can tell. Myself, I *wish* I could run out like that."

"Why don't you then?"

"Because Carlo might come home. He doesn't like me to be out. One time he was gone for three weeks and when he came home I was out. It wasn't a good thing. So, it's better that I stay."

"What do you mean? What could he—?"

She just shook her head and placed a fingertip lightly on my lips. "So what goes on at *your* house, makes you want to leave?"

Something about the warm water, the gentle scratching massage of her long nailed fingers, lulled me into honesty. "Well, every year on this weekend my criminal brother and his friends get psychotically drunk and do like rapes and beatings and vandalism and stuff at the colleges."

Felina stopped working momentarily. "Oh. I see."

"And see their headquarters is at my house and I didn't want any part of it this year, so . . ."

"Let me guess. If you're not a perpetrator, you're a victim."

"That's about the size of it, ya."

She finished washing, turned up the hot water, and rinsed me off. She worked the hose with one hand, the temperature almost high enough to hurt me, but not quite, so it felt great instead. With the other hand she gently pushed and stroked, kneading the water and soap and filth out of my hair.

I sat up straight, all combed and ready. "So how do you want it?" she asked.

I thought, and thought immediately about Ruben's look again. But he had curly hair and I didn't. He also had a thin braid running a few inches down the back of his neck.

"Cut the sides way short," I said, "and leave the back just the way it is."

"How's that?" she asked after clipping away for a few minutes.

"Shorter," I said, tilting my head and staring into the hand mirror.

"How about that?"

"Shorter."

Felina brought out the electric razor and cleaned me all around my pointy little devil ears. She shaved my sideburns up to the hairline. On top she left it medium floppy long. "Beautiful," I said. "Can you do a braid?"

Her fingers worked quickly, surely, giving little tugs on the back of my neck. I couldn't suppress a smile as I felt it coming together. When it was done, Felina pulled it around to let it lie over my shoulder in front. Even I didn't realize how long my hair had gotten, and it looked a lot longer with the sides so short. My clean new braid glistened like a skinny young red snake.

"You are awesome," I said, hopping out of the chair. I still held the mirror and swung my head side to side to let the braid slap my face. "Can I pay you or something?"

"Of course you can't," she said, shaking her head as I bounced around like a fool.

"Goddamn straight," I said to my reflection. "Oops, sorry Felina."

"Eeek, I'm shocked," she said, laughing at me again. "But where are you going to now?"

"I'm goin' *home*," I said, gritting my teeth.

"Is that a good idea?" she asked.

I shrugged, but I still felt myself grinning. "I don't know if it's a good idea, but I'm gonna find out. Is it *my* damn home, or isn't it?" I shook my fresh cut head again, frisky as a clipped dog.

Felina followed me to the door, stood on the porch drying her hands with a dish towel as she watched me trot down the stairs. "You could stay here," she said. "In Angel's room."

"Thank you very much," I said, stopping and turning to stare up at her. I wanted to then. I wanted to stay there. And I didn't want Toy to come home, and I sure didn't want big old Carlo to come home. Which was another good reason to get out of there.

But mostly I wanted, I *had* to go back to my own house. *Mine.* A guy's got to have a place, or he ain't nothin'.

"Thank you very much," I said again, "thanks for everything." Then I started my high-bounce, tail-swinging march home.

Brother Love

I heard them before I even turned the corner. They were out back barbecuing. The charred meat smell brought the reality back to me. I got a shiver. Did I really want this? No, but it wasn't as if Terry and his boys and this neighborhood and all the crap that goes along with it were ever going to go away. So what was I worth if I couldn't stand up to it?

"What the hell happened to your head?" one fat Cormac said as I reached the back porch. The Cormacs were spread out on lounge chairs flanking a giant Coleman cooler, guarding the beer like the two stone lions outside the Copley Plaza, only with bigger heads, bigger mouths, bigger bellies. Danny was passed out lying in the grass on his back. There were two middle-aged barflies from the Bloody wearing green nylon Emerald Society windbreakers, pitching horseshoes at the far end of the yard. Terry, working the grill, stared up at me as he sucked on a beer so hard it made a small whirlpool in the bottle. He was staring at my hair.

"I got me a new do," I said. "Like it?"

"Hell no," the Cormacs said.

"Hell no," Danny said, keeping his eyes closed.

"You got a call," Terry snapped as he squirted lighter fluid all over the meat on the grill, raising a three-foot flame. "Some wench named Evelyn."

I gritted. "And?"

"I told her to bring her little brown ass over to our party." He looked up at me and grinned hard.

I turned around. I thought I wanted to play. I realized now I didn't.

"Where you goin', boy?" he called.

I stopped at the door but didn't turn to face him. "I'm goin' into *my* room, in *my* house," I said.

"Don't be a damn pig!" he yelled. "You can't go in there. Frankie and Ned are in there with Honey."

I sighed. "Why my room?"

"You jokin'? I don't want that shit all over *my* sheets."

The Cormacs laughed, the old guys laughed, I heard the three people laugh from my room. The dogs Bobo and Bunky lifted their heads from where they were lying stupid under the porch and they howled.

"Hey," Terry called. "That Evelyn, she that spaniel bitch Baba told us about? You tappin' that, Mick?"

I turned now, walked down the stairs toward Terry, and got in his face. "What was that, Terry? I didn't quite hear ya."

First he laughed it off, looked over my shoulder at his laughing buddies, pretended to pretend to be scared. He took a step back and started working the grill again. I stepped up to him again, talking straight into his ear. "I said, I didn't hear you, Terry."

This time he looked up and into my eyes. Then he looked away. "Nothin', Jesus, what're you comin' in here all tense about, Mick? Jesus. Have a beer for chrissake, will ya? Jesus."

He hadn't finished talking before one of the brothers had rolled a beer across the lawn, landing it near my feet. "No thanks," I said.

Terry scooped it up. "Your loss," he said. "But

stick around anyhow, 'cause Baba and Augie are gonna be back any minute with some wicked entertainment. Relax, bro."

If ever I heard an invitation to beat feet, that was it. Terry's sudden turn into sugary snaky sweetness, the power drinking going on in all corners, combined with the million possibilities of what Baba and Augie could bring back as "wicked entertainment," reminded me quickly and finally that it was a mistake to have come back. "We missed ya," Terry said, putting his arm around my shoulder, fingering my braid.

I made like a bullet for the front of the house. I passed Honey standing by my bedroom window, her hair all sticky and matted around her round face. I was almost out of the yard when someone yelled, "They're here."

Augie came marching down along the side of the house, so blasted he didn't see me right off. "Check it out," he said, as he grabbed my arm, pulling me along with him. When we got back to the yard, everyone gathered in a circle. The Cormacs threw full beers, bullet passes bouncing off chests and cheeks to hysterical laughter and whoops. Augie crouched down and got a headlock-type grip on Bobo, stroking his boxy head and whispering in his ear.

"So where'd ya get it at?" asked Danny,

upright and full of life now with a fresh bottle of vodka in his grip.

"We grabbed it at . . . whatchacallit, that faggot art school over in the Back Bay. Just had ta give the loser spook security guard a bottle a 151 and he took a long lunch. What the hell do they need a mascot for anyway, they don't play nothin'."

Terry laughed, loud, machine-gun style, but nervous and weird. Not any kind of happy laugh. "C'mon, c'mon, c'mon," he said, waving his hands like bringing the runner home from third.

"All right," Augie said. Then he stuck two fingers in his mouth and peeled off an ear-shattering whistle. With that, Baba came lumbering down along the side of the house tugging a small white goat. A baby. Or a pygmy. Anyway, it wasn't much bigger than Bunky the Boston terrier. Baba walked the goat to the middle of the circle, and called for a horseshoe and one of the metal stakes.

"Jesus, cut the shit," I said as Baba tied off the goat's rope and hammered in the stake.

"Shut up," Augie said. Terry laughed more crazily.

"I'm not gonna let you do this," I said.

Terry must have been waiting for me to say something like that. I never even saw him move before he had grabbed my braid and slammed me, backward, to the ground. At least three of them worked on me, I don't know, but in a second I was flipped over on my belly, my chin in the dirt, with a two-hundred-sixty-pound Cormac on my back. Somebody pulled my head up by the hair, turning my face toward the action.

"Bobo, get it!" Augie screamed, and released the monster.

First, the little goat dipped his head and tried to jab the dog with his knobby blunt horns. But Bobo was running so hard all he did was just run right through him, the two of them bowling and barreling until the rope snapped tight. Bobo charged again, and the goat tried to run in the other direction, stopping short when the rope yanked his throat, choking him. He tried to keep running anyway, and even had the stake pulling loose when Bobo caught him from behind.

The big dog turned his head sideways and clamped his jaws shut across the goat's spine. He picked it up and slammed it down, first on one side, then the other. He tried to pull harder, but lost it when a big mouthful of white hair and red skin tore loose in his mouth. The goat fell and Bobo jumped him again, kicking up divots of turf as he scrambled to grab a purchase on the goat's head. He did, pinching the thin layer of flesh along the temple area, throwing him down again, turning him over to get what he wanted, what his nature told him he needed. When he grabbed the little animal's throat, Bobo was so excited he bit nearly clean through the neck.

The kicking and bucking stopped, the strangled bleating stopped, but Bobo went on, throwing the empty carcass around, biting it, snarling at it, cracking bones, tearing off pieces and letting them fall out of his mouth.

The howling, cheering, and foot stomping was so loud I could feel it through the ground under me. Honey had run crying out of the yard, but nobody else even seemed to notice.

"And now, it's Miller time," Augie yelled, and kissed his dog's bloody, frothy mouth.

What remained of the goat lay in a heap in front of me, three feet from my face. As I stared at it my eyes felt huge in my head, the weight on my back felt like nothing. Bunky came sniffing over and took a quick little lick of the goat. Abruptly, Cormac flipped me over on my back and sat back down on me, pinning my arms to my sides. Terry towered over me, his boys flanking him left and right. He drank down a whole beer in one gulp for my entertainment.

"Now ain't ya glad ya came back, Mick?"

I didn't answer.

"Ya gonna stay now? Party wid us like old times, before ya f'got who ya was?"

"Eat me."

All the boys started oooohh-ooohhing, egging Terry on to respond.

"Spit on the little fucker," somebody yelled.

"Piss on him, Terry man."

Terry smiled at that. But he did worse than that. He breathed on me. He dropped to his knees and got right in my face breathing hard. "Ya just f'get all the time lately, Mick. Ya f'get, ya can't change who ya are. You're one a us." Suddenly, like he'd been slapped, his expression changed. He didn't look like a real killer now, like he hated me. He looked weak and mushy. "You're one a *me*, remember? And ya gotta stay that way. Ya can't, like, leave. It don't work that way. We, us like, gotta stick together. Forever. I love ya, Mick, man. I love ya, I really do." There were a whole lot of yays and yas behind him. He snatched the vodka bottle out of Danny's hand. "Have a drink wit me now, brother, and we can letcha up. Then we can fix everything." He took a big, impossibly long, inhuman pull on the vodka bottle, lowered it, wiped his mouth with his sleeve, then tipped the bottle mouth down to my lips.

I kept my mouth clamped as tight as I could. I inhaled deeply and smelled the meat burned to coal on the untended grill.

"Open up," he said. He pleaded. "It's good, it's really good stuff. Stoli."

I didn't.

The killer's face returned. "Christ, *open* his hole," Terry snarled, and three sets of big hands eagerly attached to my face and pried open my jaws. I bit a finger, got a wicked slap for it. I bit again, and took knuckles across the brow. I twisted and writhed enough to almost get out from under Cormac, but then one took my hair, two more pulled my feet wide, wide apart, and my brother stuck two kerosene-drenched fingers deep into my nostrils and pulled hard upward. He stuck the bottle in my mouth and poured. I gagged, tried to spit. He covered my mouth with his hand and I swallowed. He jammed the bottle in again, way in, and while I choked, the vodka got in, and down. "I love ya, man," Terry said again and again, with that weird sad expression. I lost all fight, the bottle was in my mouth again, and vodka ran back up into my nose, out of the corners of my mouth. I coughed, I swallowed.

"I love ya, man, Mick. You're my brother. I goddamn love ya, goddammit I do. You'll see," he said. He pulled the bottle out of my mouth, took a swig, stuck the bottle back in my mouth. I thought I saw him crying before I blacked out.

I heard the rapping at my bedroom window for a while before I moved. Sounded at first like a hard wind rattling the old sash, rat-a-tat-tatting steadily for five minutes or maybe ten or thirty. Gradually, I opened one eye and made out a shadow outside the window. I opened the other and blinked, blinked fifty times trying to clear it up, but it wasn't coming. I lifted my head, but it fell back to the pillow like a million-pound melon. I started going back to sleep, and the knocking got louder and I looked up again. The gray-brown supper-time light spilled in the window from over the shadow and hurt my eyes.

I got myself off the bed, took three steps toward the window, and fell crashing to the floor. I wanted to stay down, like a fighter who wants to call it a night, but the knocking started again to urge me on. As I pushed myself up I saw that I was naked.

I made it to the window, pressed my face to the glass, and made out Toy's straw hat on the other side.

"You all right?" he asked.

I licked my cracked dry lips. They felt big

and coarse to my tongue. "I don't think so."

"Go let me in," Toy said. "Open the front door."

I shook my head. "Don't think," I said.

"What?"

"Don't think. That I can make it."

"Well, you have to make it. The front door's locked and there's a big monster dog sleeping on top of a carcass at the back door."

"Move the dog."

"*Move* the dog?"

"Ya, he's wasted I think, 'cause he does that at parties. Test his water bowl. If it tastes like vodka, just drag his ass away from the door and he won't even open his eyes."

"I think *not*," Toy said. "Go open the damn door."

"Here, I'll open the window and you can climb in." Toy just stood and watched as I feebly tried to push up the old balky window. I could barely raise my hands above my head, and the window was going nowhere.

"Open the damn door, Mick."

I nodded. "I'll try." Slowly, like a frail old man, I turned and stepped toward the door. I watched my feet shuffle over the rug, never quite lifting off the floor. I lurched forward as dizziness

119

overcame me, but managed to put a hand out in front of me to keep from smacking into my bedroom door.

When I threw the bedroom door open, I stood there looking for something, I don't know what. There appeared to be nothing out there, but then I caught the color out of the corner of my eye. All red, dripping down the outside of my door. Written with a finger, in goat's blood maybe. MICK'S SPIC CHIC SUCKS BIG DICK.

I stared at it. I couldn't think anything about it. It could have been written in Korean; there was nothing coming to me. I walked on past it, down the hall, past Terry's closed door, through the living room and the stink of Terry's unconscious friends. None moved, or even seemed to breathe, as I walked through them.

I leaned my temple against the doorway as I struggled to turn the dead bolt. The door popped open and Toy pushed through.

I stood there, naked, as he sized me up. He looked around the room, took a sniff, looked back at me. "Pretty rough haircut," he said.

Toy helped me back to my room. "This is unbelievably disgusting," he said. "It's only six thirty and they're all unconscious."

"They're gonna be up again soon. That's the

way it works. And it gets even worse—a lot worse—after that."

Toy gave me an exaggerated nod. "We have to get you out of here."

I pointed to the sign on the door as we walked into my room. He stared at it for a long time without speaking. He finally said something when he noticed me standing stupid, motionless in the middle of the room. "What's the problem?"

"Where are my clothes?" I asked, searching the floor all around me.

"I saw them in the backyard. Forget about them. You don't want 'em."

"They stripped me down outside?" I asked nobody.

When I still didn't move, Toy took over. "Sit down," he said and pushed me back onto the bed. As he rummaged through my bureau for clothes for me, I let myself fall back on the pillow. Feeling something long and hairy there, I jumped.

I turned back to look and saw it, my new braid, hacked off and left lying beside me while I was sleeping.

He had said it before, Terry. He had me, and could have me again whenever he wanted. He couldn't walk down the hall without crashing loudly into both walls, but he could come in here in my sleep and operate without my knowing. I got a shiver as I felt at the ragged bald spot on the back of my head.

"Here." Toy threw some clothes at me. "You got a bag?"

I pointed to my closet as I wrestled myself into the pants with mighty effort. Toy pulled my gym bag off the closet floor and stuffed it with clothes.

"Where are we going?" I asked, stepping gingerly into the curled-up old running shoes he threw down at my feet.

"You need a road trip," he said. "Got any money?"

I thought about it. Was there money in my pockets out in the yard? No.

"Come on, Mick. I think I heard somebody moving out there. You got any money?"

I thought again, and a smile came to me. "Yes."

I led him to Terry's room, quietly twisted the knob, and we went inside. Terry was there, in bed with his clothes on, the blankets pulled up so hard to his chin that his legs were uncovered, showing his work boots still on. The room reeked like shit, the two night tables were covered in bottles, and Terry was snoring in bursts, like a hog. Toy stood in the doorway while I went to the closet and pulled out the duffel bag crammed tight with one-dollar bills. As I eased my way past the bed again on the way out, Terry's body jerked stiff, like rigor mortis, and the snoring cut off. I froze as Terry lifted his head.

Comprehension came to him slowly, as it always did. Then he snarled at me toothy like a dog.

"I'll waste you," he said.

Just his voice shot me through with adrenaline, and I was wide awake, if a little more nauseous too. Toy took a couple of strides toward Terry, but I put out my hand to stop him.

"Come on," I said, waving Terry my way. I dropped the bag at my feet.

He smiled at me, and ponderously raised himself up on his elbows. He sat, then rolled off the side of the bed and onto his feet. He stood there for a second, still smiling his cock-ass smile at me, then suddenly looked down. He reached his hand up to the side of his head, rubbed several times, then collapsed to the floor. There he rested on the side of his head, his arms flat under him, his ass in the air.

I walked over to him. "I love ya, man," I said, and kicked him in the ribs, hard. When he rolled over, still unconscious, I kicked him again, in the stomach. He made barely a sound other than the wind shooting out his mouth. I raised my foot once more, six inches above his face, when Toy put his big hand on my shoulder and tore me away.

"I love ya, bruthaaah!" I yelled back as Toy hustled me out of the house.

When we got outside, the big Harley with the double sidecar was sitting there gleaming. "Holy smokes," I said. "This is hot shit. Hope it's fast, man, because I think we're gonna be tops on the hit parade when that party wakes back up."

"We're not going to be around," Toy said, popping a helmet on my head before thundering up the bike. It was so loud Toy couldn't hear me screaming in his ear about where we were going to go. But nobody in the house seemed to notice.

Once we were off the block, I yanked on Toy's sleeve to stop so I could puke. He pulled to the curb and cut the engine. When I finished, roaring louder than the bike, I asked where we were going.

"Going to the beach" was all he said before starting up again. I didn't even recognize it when he turned down Evelyn's street.

"What are you doin'?" I asked as he pulled up in front of the house. I was excited, but still nervous and sick.

"Picking up a rider," he said. She was already coming down the stairs.

"Hey that's right. Toy, she *called* me last night. I just remembered."

"It was this morning. And ya, I already know."

"You called me back," she said as she walked up to me in the sidecar. She looked worried as she peered down into me. "But you don't remember, do you."

"Ah . . . maybe. What did I say?"

"Nothing. A lot of gurgles and chokes. Mostly you were just crying. And there were a lot of people laughing real loud behind you."

I slinked down as low as I could into the sidecar. "Jesus Christ," I said. "Evelyn . . . I'm sorry."

"Stop it, it wasn't your fault. That was when I called Toy."

Toy laughed, finally. "Ya, my old lady was already telling me about how you looked to be cruising for trouble when you left her."

I managed to somehow slink a little bit lower into the sidecar, to where I was basically lying on the floor.

"And we'll talk about *that* situation later," Toy added. "Right now, miss, if you'll kindly hop in . . ." Evelyn pulled a helmet off the floor of the front section of the sidecar. She threw her bag in.

I was sitting, stunned, right behind her. "You're *coming*? On the road trip?"

"You're a needy boy, Mick," Toy cut in. "And a damn lucky one, I might add. I may be a chauffeur, but I'm no nurse. Evelita's a good soul."

"Shut up and drive," Evelyn said.

I felt so good for that one moment, as the Harley engine caught and rattled my fillings, that I couldn't form words. My head lolled back and I looked straight up at the sunset sky as we peeled away under it.

Part Two

Part Two

Refugee

Like Toy said, they took me to the beach. But not just any beach. We rode about an hour and a quarter up I-95 to the short strip where New Hampshire's toe touches the Atlantic. I had been there before, but like most people I had been there in the summer. In the off-season it was a different place, a place where lowlifes and weirdos, drifters and criminals came to relax and be invisible. My father once told me that Charles Manson and Carlos the Jackal spent winters in Hampton Beach. And now me. Perfect.

But it wouldn't have mattered to me where it was. I slept the whole ride up, revived briefly to be led up the motel steps, then crashed face-down on the bed as soon as I reached the room. When I finally woke the next morning, it took me half an hour to piece it all back together and remember where on the map I'd landed. To tell the truth, it took me that long to even care where I was. Because I was there with Evelyn.

I lay in the bed, scooted up behind her. Not touching her anywhere, but close enough so I could feel the heat of her all along our lengths. I arranged myself to be bent just like she was, lying sideways in kind of an S-curl tuck, shadowing, not touching her. The front of my knees an inch away from the back of her knees. My stomach an inch from the small of her back. My nose just touching her hair.

Then she quietly slipped out of bed, barely rustling the covers. She stood up—wearing her sweatshirt, jeans, and socks—and turned back toward me.

"Oh," she said. "You're awake. Feeling all right?"

I nodded, and a smile broke out. "I feel pretty great."

"Amazing."

"I have to ask, Evelyn. Did we . . . you know, did we *do* stuff?"

She stared at the ceiling and rubbed her forehead, as if she had my hangover.

"Well, *I* didn't, but you, you did lots of stuff. You drooled. You snored. And one time you fell out of the bed."

"Oh," I said, disappointed.

Evelyn sat down on the one chair under the one window in the tiny room. There was just enough space for it and the bed, with the bamboo pattern wallpaper making the walls seem even closer. She began putting on her sneakers.

"Look, Mick, I wanted to help you out here; don't let your imagination run wild."

Her big eyes were softer now, the puffiness of sleep still there. My insides were getting all confused, with all that had happened, and I knew I was attaching too much to Evelyn. I was stung with the sudden sinking feeling, of how temporary this all was. The feeling sped up, and pulled me along. Was it a joke? Was she just going to dump me here and vanish? I would, if I were her. What was I going to be left with after this?

Now I didn't trust *Evelyn*.

"What's the deal?" I asked. "Why are you doing this?"

"Toy asked me to," she said evenly. "I respect Toy."

"That's not enough."

"You remind me of my dad."

"*Now* we're getting somewhere," I said.

131

"He was a loser too. He's dead now, though."

I quit there. I wasn't up to hearing any more of that, so I didn't ask for any more.

After she'd finished tying her laces, Evelyn came over and sat on the bed.

"It seemed to me you could use a friend. Toy had to bring the bike back, he didn't really want to leave you here alone. And I figured after that horrible phone call that maybe you're not so much a loser as you are unlucky."

I looked at her silently. She shrugged, and smiled.

"Okay?" she offered.

"Okay," I accepted.

We spent the day killing time until Toy came back to get us. We ate breakfast in the bar on the first floor of the motel, then went for a long walk on the deserted beach. We carried our shoes and walked the water's edge where the waves came flattening out around our feet and the sand was cold and hard and pounded smooth as a tabletop. We spun and walked backward for a long ways, just to do it, because we could. Walked for ten minutes without bumping into anyone. I stared down the beach northways and couldn't see anything. I flipped back around and the whole south was ours alone too. Out to the east, over the water, there was one lone bump of a lobster boat on the horizon but otherwise, there seemed to be nothing between us and England. It occurred to me that this may have been the first thing that Evelyn and I both appreciated, this solitude. We walked in silence for a mile in each direction.

We finally left the beach for the boulevard in the afternoon when we started getting hungry. We ate pizza, drank Cokes, slipped into the arcade to play a few games. We acted like kids, and pretended for as long as we could that all the other stuff wasn't out there.

"You thinking about where you're going to go?" Evelyn finally asked as the afternoon wound down.

I waved her on out of the arcade so we could start back down the boulevard to the motel. "No," I said. "I mean, no, I don't *think* I'm thinking about it, like, I don't hear words in my head the way I usually do when I'm thinking about something."

"No, I didn't see your lips moving either."

I didn't mind anymore that she was making fun of me. But I didn't laugh.

"Well, I don't hear the words, haven't heard any actually since we got here. But I'm *feeling* stuff, you know? And so, ya, I think somewhere in there I'm thinking about where I'm going but

I'm not telling myself." I waited a few seconds, slowed my walk to almost nothing, then said, "Y'know?" the way you say it when you're sure nobody knows.

I was afraid to look at her face, and when she didn't say anything I got all embarrassed, started walking fast again. "Never mind," I said. "Don't listen to me. I'm a dope."

We bought pineapple-banana whips and fat oily fried doughs, the powdered sugar soaking up the oil and making little balls on the top. We took them back to the motel and sat on the swing eating them, waiting for Toy. It was getting cloudy and misty, the wind from the ocean bearing in and leaving us coated in cold salty spray.

"I should probably go check out," I said. "You want to wait here?"

She nodded, staring off into the rough, incoming tide.

Upstairs I pulled the chair to the window, and sat staring out with my chin on my hands. I saw those waves way off again but coming closer, and still loud through the closed window. The delicious salt wind rattling the old loose sash. I could see why refugee types would come to this town. Twenty-four hours or so had sure made me feel I was in the right place. I wondered if this was where Toy came on all those field trips.

The peace was shattered, though, when I felt the rumble of the engine through the crash of the waves. I grabbed the bags and left reluctantly. Downstairs I paid the front desk lady with bills from the bag I'd stolen from my brother.

Toy was on the swing with Evelyn when I stepped out onto the porch.

"I don't ever want to leave here," I said. "I'm never going to leave here." I looked past him, up and down the silent boulevard, loving it, meaning what I was saying. The thought that this perfect windswept world and that vile little place I'd bolted existed so close together and that I could choose to be in either one of those worlds . . . well, that thought was too big for me. It steamrolled me.

"Yes you are, Mick, you're going back," he said. "Come Memorial Day, you couldn't afford a week here. And I hope you've thought about this: You can't stay here, and you sure can't go back home. So where you gonna go?"

"Maybe I could go to your house? For a while?"

"Maybe you can't," Toy answered, not mean, but firm anyway.

"How come? Your mother did—"

"Because my life is my life. And while we're on the subject, stop sniffing around my mother."

I turned to Evelyn. Hopefully.

She smiled sympathetically. "Maybe we better count that bag of money and see what you can afford."

I had no place.

Toy fired up the Harley.

The ride home down the wide open of route 95 seemed to take no time at all. Sixty-five miles to go, said the sign. Then, suddenly, twenty-five. At every mile marker my stomach tightened a little more, fear and a thumping anger hitting me from sights unseen and unexpected until, by the time we were in the city, I was pumping my jaw like there was a wad of gum in my mouth.

Toy looked at me for the answer to the question he hadn't asked.

I pointed. A left here, a left there, a right here, all the way to the end, then another left. I still hadn't thought it out, still hadn't heard the words in my head, but I suppose I just already knew. Toy pulled in front of the house and I got out. I couldn't say anything, couldn't even say thanks. But it didn't seem to bother either of them. I waved. They waved.

My decision after all was no decision at all. Where did I always go? When Terry cooked frozen eggrolls at three A.M., nodded off, and the firemen came because of the smoke, where did I go? When my mother was away and my father forgot to come home from the O'Asis and the lights went out all over the block, and I was only nine, where did I go? When they had given my bed away to yet another late guest and I couldn't bear to sleep on the couch because sleeping out in the open spooked me, where did I go? When I was older and I couldn't sleep because it was New Year's Eve and my parents' friends couldn't stop screaming over and over the only five words they knew from "Auld Lang Syne," where did I go?

I didn't even have to whistle or ring the bell. The motorcycle noise brought Sully to the door. He stared at me hard.

"S'pose you heard things," I said.

"S'pose I did," he answered.

"So, will you take me?"

I never had to ask before, just walked in when the door opened.

He didn't stop looking at me hard.

"No." He slammed the door in my face.

I had no idea in the world where I was walking to when I turned away from that door. There was no bottom for me now.

The door flew back open.

"Get in, asshole," he said.

He just left the door open and walked away

from it, back into the house. A combination invitation-slap. Inside he continued on, through the hall and up the stairs toward his room. I followed at a distance, looking this way and that for anybody else, his parents, or Honey. The place was empty.

Upstairs, Sully walked to the door that led to the attic, right next to his own bedroom door, and threw it open the same unfriendly way he did the front door. Then he went into his room.

I took the hint. Instead of messing with Sully yet, I took my bag up the second flight of stairs to the attic. To the guest room. To my old room. Sully's parents actually own their house, and a long time ago fixed up the attic for guests. It even has its own bathroom except that they never quite finished it so the toilet is still just the drain pipe opening up out of the floor. It works fine, though, as long as you don't get too sloppy. The bedroom part of the attic is a little cramped with the slope ceilings and the two single beds tucked into the eaves at either end, but it is comfortable. There's a thick brown carpet, night tables next to each bed, and pictures of the Kennedys looking like backlit angels on the wall. And a couple of those fifties floor lamps, spring rods that are pressed between the floor and the ceiling, with four cone-shaped lights pointing in every which direction. There's only one tiny radiator, and the place is drafty as hell, but with the thick rug, with the calico down comforter on the bed, with a couple of those lamps trained just right throwing that yellow light, there was a lot more warm about it than cold. I remembered that from every time I stayed there before. It was doubly true this time.

So it wasn't such a hard place to kill some time even though it was eerie quiet and the two dwarf doors that opened to the crawl spaces were spooking me. I couldn't do that forever, though. I had to go down and see him.

I stood in his doorway. He lay flat on his bed, his eyes closed.

"Um, thanks," I said.

"Don't," he said, nasty.

"You want me to leave?"

"Up to you."

"Why'd you let me in?"

"Why'd you come?"

"'Cause this is where I come. You know that."

"This is where you *used* to come."

"Then why did I come?"

"Then why did you come?"

"Then why'd you let me in?"

"'Cause I'm a dope, I guess."

"You are, but that don't answer the question."

"Then I don't know the answer."

"Yes you do."

"Shut up, I said I don't."

"Well I do. I know why you let me in."

"Oh that's right. You know every damn thing now, dontcha?"

"Not every damn thing, but some."

"So?"

"So, you let me in because . . ." I felt it building, didn't want it to, but couldn't stop it. "You let me in because you love me, Sul."

Without opening his eyes, he reached back over his head and grabbed a tall green Tupperware cup full of water off the night table and winged it at me. "Get outta my goddamn house," he yelled as the cup bounced and splattered off the door and I ran.

But I didn't run out of the house. I ran upstairs to my room. Because I knew he didn't mean it.

I flopped down on my bed and was asleep before I could even kick my shoes off. I don't know how long I slept, only that I could have slept a lot longer if the light hadn't woken me. When I heard the click and saw the lamp glowing pink through my eyelids, I opened them to see Sully's father, John J. Sullivan II, hulking over me. I was startled, but I didn't jump or yell or gasp. My startle muscles didn't seem to work anymore.

Besides, I liked Mr. Sullivan. Mostly because he had basically no use for anybody at all. He looked like the actor Sean Connery, big, about six-three, half bald, with a thick gray mustache and hands like catcher's mitts with fingers added on.

Mr. Sullivan had only turned on one of the lights, and aimed it right at me. So he was kind of lurking in the shadow behind it.

"Hey, Mr. Sullivan."

"Hey, Mick."

I could see him smiling a know-everything grin.

"Y'ain't been to stay with us in a long time. Nice ta see ya."

"Nice ta be back," I said.

"Your old man called. Ya know I can't stand your old man, dontcha, Mick?"

"Ya, I know."

"But I listened to him anyway. He asked was you here and I told him ya, you was. So he says, okay."

"Okay? Okay what? Does he want me to come right home? Does he want me to call?"

Mr. Sullivan shrugged the big beefy shoulders. "Okay, he says."

I nodded, thought about getting up, standing, sitting, *something* that required action. But then I couldn't think of a reason, so I didn't move.

"There's a little refrigerator in the basement," he said, walking away. "I'll bring it up." He disappeared down the stairs, then suddenly reappeared, walking backward up the same stairs. "But Mick, if I find any beer in it I'll throw your ass out on the street. Right?"

I gulped. "Right."

In a few minutes he was back, carrying the small square refrigerator in front of him like it was a shoebox. He set it down in the corner, plugged it in. "Now this doesn't mean you can't come down and eat with us if you want sometimes. It's just . . . well, you don't have to if you don't want to, is all."

He really doesn't like people very much.

As soon as Mr. Sullivan was back down the stairs, I heard Sully coming up. His footsteps were a lot lighter. He stood near the top of the stairs for a few seconds, his thin face peering through the bannister.

"Comin' in?" I asked.

He did. He walked to the other bed, the one

across the room from me, flicking on the light closest to it. He spread out on his bed on his side, just like me on mine. We lay there, each floating in our narrow cone of light.

"I feel like I don't know you now, Mick."

"Good."

"Why? Why is that good?"

"Because I'm not the same anymore. My house, my family, my rotten neighborhood, I ain't a part of that anymore, Sul. I just can't connect myself to it. So I guess if you want to know me again, you have to *get* to know me."

There was a long silence while Sully worked on that.

"I don't like it. Don't like the sound of it, Mick. You're really sounding kinda fulla shit lately. Like you really do think you're better than everybody."

"I am," I blurted.

Sully hopped up off his bed. "You suck, man."

"Wait a minute, wait a minute," I said, sitting up now. "That's not what I meant exactly."

"I'm listening," Sully said, folding his arms and refusing to sit back down. "But not for long."

"Well, I'm better than Terry, that's what I mean."

"No shit, Sherlock, who isn't?"

"Us, you and me. We didn't used to be any better than him. Baba ain't no better than him. And think about this: You see what an animal Baba is? Well, we all were like, *best friends* not too long ago. Y'know, it looks like there's a zillion miles between him and us, but really, there ain't much at all. Here's my problem, Sul. I can't stop seeing that anymore. I can't look at anyone around me without seeing Baba, and me. And Terry, and me. And Augie, and me . . ."

"And Sully, and you? That what you're sayin'? Old friend?"

"No," I said, weakly.

"Yes it is. I gotta tell ya, Mick, the superiority thing doesn't make you sound so great."

"I know," I said. I was up on my knees now, talking more urgently to him. I had the feeling of a stakes now, of something I had to get done. I was losing Sully here, and I was all of a sudden convinced—desperately—that I couldn't lose Sully.

"I know I sound like a shit, but I don't care. I *am* better than those sons of bitches and I can say it because for the first time *ever* I feel it. I feel like I'm better than someone."

Now a lighter expression bloomed across Sully's face. He nodded smartly. "Ohhh, I get it. You got laid, didn't ya?"

"No, no, no, no, no, no, no, Sully, you stu-pid—"

"I'm leavin'," he said.

"Don't," I pleaded.

"Mick, I gotta go. All I wanna know is, where are we at, me and you? Huh? You outgrown me too?"

I opened my mouth to answer twice before anything came out. The third try, something came out.

"I don't know," I said.

"That's a great answer, friend."

"Well, I guess it depends on what you want to be. You can't be partway ignorant, Sully, that much I know."

"I ain't ignorant," he said.

"I believe that's the truth."

"But I won't pretend I'm not who I am. Like you're doing."

"Bullsh—"

He stuck out both hands in front of him, like a traffic cop. "Maybe this is good enough for now, huh? You said a little something, I said a little something, that should hold us for a while. This naked truth shit is starting to make my brain hurt."

"Fine, as long as you understand things are

gonna be changing around here, big time."

Sully headed back toward the stairs, shaking his head. "You know I don't like change, man. You know that."

"Cambio está bueno," I said.

"Don't start with me," he growled, then disappeared through the floor.

I was left there again, alone. I paced. I had nowhere to go, nothing to do. Nothing. I paced my A-shaped room with nothing but that thought in my mind.

Sully poked his head back up. "You gonna come down and eat, or what? The old man says you better not go expectin' this all the time, but. . . . He really likes you, actually."

I was happy, walking down the stairs behind Sully, though I knew Mr. Sullivan meant it.

"And one more thing," Sully said, without turning back to face me, without slowing down, trying to sound as casual as he could. "If you ever say that thing to me again—that thing, the one you said in my room, about why I let you in—if you ever say that thing to me again, I'll get the old man's handgun—and it's a goddamn cannon—and I swear I'll put you away."

He made me laugh, which felt awfully good. "So then it's true," I said.

"I'll kill ya right now, waste ya right at the dinner table in front of my parents and everything."

"Okay," I said, not laughing anymore but smiling hard. "I won't mention it again, Sul."

Cambio

Sully and I headed out together in the morning, back to school, like a couple of brothers. Like when we were kids. I was even wearing his clothes, a red-and-white-striped oxford shirt, stiff dark-blue jeans, and loafers. Most of my stuff was still at . . . the other house.

"Y'know, Sul, I think it's only fair to tell you, I'm probably going to be a little too popular these days, with Terry and Augie and Baba."

"I know," he said. He tried to look brave, tried to swagger a bit as he walked by my side. But I could see his tightened white lips. "Not a problem," he said, staring straight ahead.

"What I'm trying to say is, I'll understand if you don't—"

He shook his head a million times in a second, like the beat of a hummingbird's wings. "New subject. Something else," he said.

I let it go, impressed with his take on bravery. And, in a short while he seemed to have forgotten about it and returned to what he was before—happy to have me back. In a few minutes, he started smiling, to himself.

"What?" I asked, forced to smile along with him.

"Baba, at least, ain't gonna be a problem for ya. Not for a while anyway. Not for, oh, about twenty-eight days."

"Detox? Sully, Baba's in *detox*? You're joking."

He shook his head, giggling. "Nope. His old man stuck him in down at Edgehill. Seems that toward the end of May Day weekend Baba came home a little mental and killed their dog." Sully stopped and did a shudder, a full-body wiggle. "Hear it was pretty grim, Baba chewin' the dog up and shit."

I burst out laughing, without feeling particularly amused.

"So," he said, slapping my back, "it's early summer vacation for old Baba."

I let out a sigh at those words. Suddenly,

school was a better place, without the guy who was once my protector. Sully felt it too. He bopped around a lot, joked, punched me when he talked, acting like a little kid allowed to tag along with his big brother.

"Whoa, watch out for him," he said, clearing a path for me up the school steps. "He's better than you are, y'know."

"Shut up," I said.

"Hey, he's homeless, but he's still better than you are," he called down the hall to the principal, who ignored him like he does all students.

It shot through me when he said that. "Stop calling me homeless, Sully."

"That's right, I forgot. You have a home, you just don't live there."

"Have I told you lately to shut up? Shut up."

Thank god nobody listens to the guy. He just kept laughing and telling the world the great joke that I was better than them. Until we came to the group, outside Evelyn's homeroom. Evelyn, Toy, and Ruben. Then he shut up.

Seeing us approach from a long way, the three of them stood taking us in. Evelyn smiled and nodded approvingly. Ruben frowned. Toy showed *nada*.

"Well hello, John," Evelyn said to Sully.

At first he didn't react, probably because he hadn't been called John in so long he'd forgotten it was him. Then he gave her a ratty rotten fake smile.

"So, I guess that's it for me," he said to me, and started walking toward our homeroom. Sully was still having trouble with the change thing, still stuck with the old neighborhood crap that said a guy was either on one side or the other. He couldn't decide if I'd sold out by hanging around with Toy and Ruben.

"*Adiós,*" Ruben said, waving at Sully's back.

I watched that back for a few seconds as he walked away.

"Sully," I called. He waved without turning around. "Sully." This time he didn't even wave. It's just going to take time, I thought. He's slow, but he's not ignorant.

"They was only jokin' me, right?" Ruben crashed in. "You isn't really *livin'* wit dat Sullivan dick, are you?"

I looked back down the hall where Sully was, then back to Ruben. "Ya, I am. For now. You know. And he ain't a dick."

"Leave him alone, Ruben, will you?" Evelyn asked. "I think it makes total sense."

I looked at her, felt the stupids coming over

me, looked at Toy again. Toy shrugged. "Your life, man. It's got to be better than what you had before."

"It is. It sure is that," I said.

"It's just good that you're here. That you're *somewhere*. That your life makes a bit of sense." Evelyn paused. "For a change."

"Cambio," Toy kicked in.

"Ya, for a change," Ruben chimed, cackling loud and phonylike. He leaned to Toy. "What's the change, again? He don't look no different to me, 'cept he got some stupid-lookin' whitey clothes on."

I had Sully's *clothes* on, even. Sully gave me his *clothes*.

Evelyn gave my hand a tug, but looked at her brother. "It's an internal change, a psychic change. This is a man on the move, a brave man you're looking at, Ruben, a free man."

"Oh no, look out boys, they's a poem comin' this way. Duck!"

Toy laughed, Ruben ducked, I just stared at Evelyn with, I think, a "Huh?" look on my face. She recited.

> *"It's little I care what path I take,*
> *And where it leads it's little I care;*
> *But out of this house, lest my heart break,*
> *I must go, and off somewhere."*

By the time she finished, my heart was thrumming, scared, and awed with Evelyn, with the kind of inside stuff she knew, and with the control she had over it. I thought, What a help that must be, to know the words that make everything make sense.

Ruben was gone after two lines. Toy, his hat pulled a little lower than usual, smiled.

"Edna St. Vincent Millay," he said.

I reeled further. "How many languages do you two speak that I don't?"

"Including English?" he laughed, slapped my cheek, and took off. "Catch you later," he said.

When it was just the two of us left, Evelyn put a hand on my arm. "I'm glad you're living with John," she said. "Everyone should have someone who loves them at home."

"Oh, I had that where I lived before," I said. "Terry told me he loved me as he was pushing a bottle neck down my throat."

She didn't answer that one. She just nodded, motioned toward her classroom, and went in. I was standing in the corridor alone when the bell clanged to start classes. I reached homeroom just as Sully was leaving.

"What, are you going to have to lead a double life now, one with me, and one with them?"

"Hey, you're the one who left," I said.

"And you're the one who let me."

"Sul, you're invited to go everywhere I go, do everything I do. I don't make no separation here; if you do, then you're the one who's separating. But don't make me chase you, 'cause I won't."

Then he walked away from me, again, and I let him, again. He couldn't be pushed to do anything. But I had faith in him. If I ever believed that he really would separate from me, I wouldn't have brought it up.

It may have been my imagination, my mood, or it may have been true, but I didn't make contact with anybody throughout the school day. I floated into a class, sat there, heard nothing, and floated back out again. Nobody registered, nobody talked to me, nobody touched me. I had stuff taught to me, words thrown my way, but none of it rooted. I was thinking something, something else, but I didn't know what it was. My thoughts were thinking without me.

"I gotta go home," I blurted, a lump of tuna rolling out of my mouth because I didn't realize it was there.

Toy sat across the cafeteria table from me, eating nothing, as usual. "Yuck, man, why would you want to go there?" he asked, remembering the putrid situation he'd rescued me from.

"I gotta get my stuff."

"Hell, Mick, I frankly don't think your stuff was all that great. Certainly not good enough to go back there. You look fine in what you're wearing."

"Because it's *my* stuff," I growled. "I ain't no fuckin' refugee, Toy. I left there 'cause I *wanted* to. That's *my* stuff, goddamnit, I can't not get it. I can't let that happen to me."

Toy said nothing. He wanted to, I knew, but he couldn't. Because he felt the same way about things. Nobody kicked *his* ass out of anywhere.

As he sat waiting for my next move, or word, I sat not knowing what it was. Sully walked by, brown bag in hand. He looked us up and down, then walked on.

I jumped up and grabbed him by the arm. He shook me off. I hugged him and wrestled him down into the seat next to me.

"Toy, this is Sully," I said.

"I know."

"And Sully's been my best friend since we were little kids and even though he's confused and stupid sometimes and we aren't exactly alike anymore like we used to be, he still is. And sometimes I forget, but that doesn't change it any. My best friend. You have any problem with that?"

He sighed. "Like I said, it's your life, Mick."

I was still hugging Sully hard enough to pinch his shoulders together, afraid he'd bolt.

"That girl's made you a total sap. Let go of me, wouldja?" he said, and wriggled free. He stared across the table at Toy, then looked down and started pawing at his lunch bag.

There was a long uneasy silence, then Toy said, to Sully, "He says he's going back to his house. To get his stuff."

Sully's head whipped my way. He opened his mouth wide, with a mouthful of Fluffernutter. "What're you, stupid?" he garbled. "Wear my clothes, they look great on ya. Look a whole lot better than Terry's boots'll look on your throat."

That was it. I stood up. "I'm gone," I said.

"Right now?" Toy and Sully said simultaneously.

"It can't wait," I said.

They stared at each other.

Slowly, incredibly, Sully stood up. He stepped away from the table, toward me.

"Finish your lunch first," I said.

He shook his head. "Can't. Feel like I'm gonna puke now."

He certainly couldn't be much help, but I was glad to have him. I gave Toy a salute, and started leading Sully out of the caf. He was a little hunched over already.

"Jesus *Christ*!" Toy yelled, like a father, as he followed.

When we got to the house, I stood on the steps looking up at the door. The two of them stood a few feet behind me.

"He won't be in there. He works, right?" Toy asked.

"I really think I'm gonna be sick," Sully moaned. "You don't need to go in, I just got some new sweaters for my birthday . . . they always give me sweaters . . . I never wear them . . ."

I didn't go in. I turned, brushed by them, and went around to the back. By the time Toy caught up to me, I was on my hands and knees in the grass, looking at it. Trying to remember the little shredded May Day goat. If it really could have happened.

"You all right?" he asked.

"Goat's blood."

"Excuse?"

"The brown stuff here, it came out of a goat."

He stared down at me as I snuffled around like a mole.

"Mick, what are we doing here? You look insane, man. Get up."

He stuck out his hand and pulled me up. Sully came tearing into the yard, waving his arms and desperately trying to yell and whisper at the same time.

"I saw a move I saw a move I saw a move, goddamnit, I saw a move. Let's get outta here."

"Sully, don't make me slap you," I said. "What did you see?"

"A move. I saw a move. In the house. In your room, I think. Somebody opened the curtain, and closed it again quick. He's here, goddamnit, he's here. How could you do this to me, god-damnit, let's get the—"

"It's probably just my mother, Sul."

"Uh-uh. It *ain't* your mother. I only caught a peek, but it ain't her."

I felt my face flush. I made a fist, opened it again, curled it, opened it. I found myself rising up on the balls of my feet.

"What's in it for you?" Toy asked sternly.

I barely heard him. "Huh?"

"This isn't going to do you any good. This is a loser game, Mick. I don't think you should go in."

"Ya, I don't think so either, don't think you should, don't think you should, don't think so," Sully reasoned.

"You can wait, or you can leave," I said, stomping around to the front door.

They followed me, closer than before. Even Sully was hanging tight, even if he was making little nervous whimper noises under his breath.

I stuck my key in the door, turned it, then swung around to Toy. I pointed my finger in his face.

"Don't let me die," I said. "But short of that, this is not your problem, it's mine."

He didn't answer. He understood.

I swung the door open and stood staring in, like the cops do on TV when they go into a criminal's place. Nothing happened, so I stepped in.

"Ma?" I said hopefully.

"Please, oh please answer," Sully whispered.

Nothing. The house seemed normal as I stepped through. The front hall, the living room, the dining room. They were all the way they were when I still lived there. Terry and friends had put back all the overturned furniture, replaced the broken glass, sawdusted the vomit, grilled the scattered goat pieces—if they even bothered to cook it before eating—and let the dogs gnaw the bones down to unrecognizable nothing. It was all gone now, because it was Monday. And they were back to being carpenters and pipe fitters and telephone workers going

159

into people's houses and saying "Yes, ma'am" and "Thank you, ma'am" and "Sure, a Pepsi would be great because, y'know, a guy sure does get thirsty on a job like this" and "Yes, sir, it's a dirty shame what's become of the Celtics since Bird and McHale retired. Disgusting, can't even watch 'em no more."

They were good at what they did. They ravaged like Hell's Angels, then they swept up like Merry Maids. There were only the two messy details. One was me, and I actually did them a favor by removing myself. The other was the smell. The smell of the booze saturating the place, seeping into the rugs, of dogs too drunk to remember to go outside, of beer-bellied psychopaths who don't bathe all weekend and who can't wait for the bathroom line so they piss in the kitchen sink. Try as he might, over the years, Terry never found a way to deal with that smell so it hung there for two or three or four weeks, haunting that house with its sickness until it faded.

I shook my head and gagged at the same time as I smelled the whole can of potpourri air freshener my mother had lamely layered on top of it all.

Sully and Toy hovered in the front doorway for a while, but when I headed for the bedrooms, Toy came up behind me. Terry's door was open.

The room was empty. For a second I thought I was going to cry as I approached his bed. I stood there, looking down on where he'd be. The same spot where I last saw his drunk, evil, unhuman ass. I kicked the bed, like I'd kicked his ribs. I kicked it again.

I felt Toy's presence back there. I wasn't sure where he was. But I knew he was close.

"I *would* have killed him, Toy. I would have done it."

His voice came from a couple of feet back. "And I would have let you. If I thought you could get away with it."

Across the hall, we heard the noise. In my bedroom.

"Shit," Toy said. It was the first time I'd ever seen him really surprised.

"Shit," Sully echoed from way off. "Shit. Shit."

I pushed by Toy and threw open the door to my room.

Like a hairy brown missile, the beast threw itself at me without a sound. I yanked the door shut just in time for him to crash against it.

Sully had run out the front door already, and was peeking back in.

"What is it?" Toy asked, angrily, like what-ever the hell it was, he wanted to fight it.

"It's a goddamn dog, I think," I said, my

161

chest inflating and deflating with terror. I listened with my back to the door as the thing scratched and pawed around, then stopped. I cracked the door and peeked in.

He sat curled on the floor under the window, the curtain hanging above him chewed to pieces. He raised his arrow-shaped head toward me and curled one lip to snarl without sound. My bedposts were chewed to splinters. There was a fresh shit in the middle of the rug. My stereo cabinet was tipped over and my bedspread was on the floor, covered with dog hair. I closed the door quietly.

"It looks like part Doberman, part shepherd," I said. "It's got paws the size of baseballs." I leaned my forehead against the door. "He got himself a damn dog, and he gave it my room. And they *let* him."

"Come on," Sully said. He'd actually come all the way in now, and stood right behind me. "Come on, Mick. Let's go home."

I smiled at that—for the moment liked the sound of it. I stepped back from the door. My door. And there it was. Scrubbed, but still there. A watery pink blur now, but still plenty to remind me of the bloody note he'd left me.

"Not yet," I said, and stormed back to Terry's room. I went right for the top drawer of his bureau, underneath the twelve pairs of white socks with the green and yellow rings around the calf. I pulled out his bottle of Bushmills, the real thing, that he got on his trip to Ireland. I uncapped it.

"Oh, Mick, you don't really want to do that, do you?" Toy asked.

I smiled at him, then upended the bottle, pouring great brown spirals out on the already stained mattress.

"Yee-hah," Sully said, clapping excitedly like one of those wind-up monkeys with cymbals.

"But is he even going to notice?" Toy laughed.

I got more wired. I did more. I had to do more. There wasn't enough.

I whipped it out. I pissed in the bottle.

It grew in my hand, I was so mental excited. I almost couldn't get the right stuff out, but I did, filling the bottle about a third full. I capped the bottle and put it back in the drawer, closed the drawer, and fell to the floor laughing.

I laughed alone. Sully stared at me with a scared look. Toy stayed cool.

"And I'll say it again," he said. "Will he even know the difference?"

I laughed and laughed and laughed.

"Tell me something, Mick. Pissing in a bottle,

did that make you feel like you got what you came for? Like you're better than he is?"

I kept laughing, sitting there on the floor, almost crying. "No. It didn't."

I stopped laughing. "Sully, go get a couple of bags," Toy said.

Sully went to the kitchen and came back with two shopping bags.

"What did you come here for, Mick?" Toy asked. "Come on, take what's yours, man."

I got up, remembered the dog in my old room, and almost sat down again. Then it came to me. Terry's bureau was right at my back. I spun and started pulling open drawers.

He has about twenty pairs of new jeans. He wears two of them. I took ten. I took shirts. I took the two pastel sweatshirts my mother bought when she read that article on colors and aggression control. He'd thrown them at her. Socks and underwear? I'd buy new ones with the money I stole from him. I went to the closet, took a London Fog raincoat he bought when he was drunk in the rain down by Filene's on payday. I took the pair of white leather cross-trainers that he stole from *me* and then didn't ever wear. "Sully, more bags," I called.

"Sully, more bags," Toy echoed.

"More bags," Sully sang.

When we'd filled up, we put the bags on the floor outside the room. I felt good, but I wasn't quite sure yet. "Am I finished?" I asked Toy. He shook his head.

"Sullivan, come here," Toy said, motioning Sully to the foot of the bed. Toy grabbed the headboard and they lifted, carrying the bed to the other side of the room. Then they moved the bureau to the corner where the bed was. The foot locker they hauled over to beneath the window.

"Yes," I said, and ran to the living room. I came back with a long cushion from the couch, laying it across the foot locker to make a nice window seat.

"Very Terry," I said, beaming.

They howled. "Very Terry, very Terry," we all chanted as we finished redecorating.

"Got any paint?" Sully asked. He froze in the middle of the room, as if he'd shocked even himself.

"Of *course*," I said, and flew down to the cellar. All I could find were a blue-gray can of Rustoleum spray and a quart of burnt-orange latex with a rock-hard brush my mother used to keep painting over the mold strip around the tub. I threw the Rustoleum to Sully. "You're up," I said.

He barely hesitated. Making as large a circle

as his reach would allow, he painted a peace sign on the wall opposite the bed, where Terry would be facing it when he woke up. Then he did a butterfly.

"*Very* Terry," I said, clapping.

Toy was already working. He'd grabbed the burnt-orange away, stood on the dirty clothes–covered chair, and was painting a huge sunrise over, beside, and below the window, with the window itself as the center. It looked like the mural covering the entire back of the supermarket near Toy's house—where the ponytail christ-guy of exploding colors stretches his arms wide under an orange sun just like that one with spiky triangular rays detached from the ball.

As Toy was finishing the last of the triangle rays, I took the Rustoleum can and made my contribution, to the wall right beside the bed. I was as surprised as anyone when I saw the picture of the goat coming out on the wall. It was primitive, like a cave-wall goat. But it was a goat. The can sputtered as I rushed to get it finished before the paint dried up.

The three of us stood crunched together in the doorway, admiring it. In a weird way, we had made a pretty place out of the room.

"Very Terry." Sully spat.

"He'll come home wasted," I said, "maybe

grab a last swallow of Bushmills Old Urine, then try to fall into bed, and break his nose on the floor. He won't even know where he is."

"Time, gentlemen," Toy the dad said.

We each scooped a couple of bags of my new wardrobe and headed out. I was the last.

"Time," Toy called, from out on the porch now.

"Ya," I said. But the phone rang. I stared at it. It rang again, rang *at* me. I put a bag down and grabbed the receiver.

I heard the unmistakable breathing. The whistle through the one clear nostril left from all the nose breakings. The low animal pant. He waited a long time.

"Ma?" he grunted.

I let him hang some more.

"Welcome to the homeless," I whispered as softly as a person can.

I hung up and walked out, butterflies of satisfaction beating in my belly.

O'Asis

I had been at Sully's for four days, eating, sleeping, going to school, and staring for long hours out my dormer window, before I got a call.

"Yo, ah, Mick," Mr. Sullivan called from the bottom of the stairs. "Your ma's on the horn for ya."

I took my time getting to the phone. I straightened out the curtain over the window I'd been staring out of. I pulled on my sneakers, then changed my mind and decided to go without them. I counted the steps between my room, my suite, my bungalow—my pointed penthouse, there ya go—and the floor below. Thirteen steps.

That sounded odd. So I retraced and counted again. Yup, thirteen. I washed my hands in the second-floor bathroom.

I wanted to hear her cry, but I could wait.

"Why are you not home yet, Mick? I mean, a couple of days is fine, but this is enough now. Come on home today, after school."

I laughed, not to be rude, though not that I minded. "Ma. I mean, thanks for missing me, but no thanks, okay?"

"What's the problem, Mick? Please just come home, today. All right, I'll see you later then, right?"

She didn't want any answers, any explanations. Not really. She just wanted everything put back, straightened up. As if I'd just messed up the living room or something.

"No, Ma, you just don't get it. I'm not coming back there. I cannot live with that animal anymore."

"Mick!" Only very rarely did her voice rise to the level of a cough, so I listened. "That 'animal' has slaved to put a roof over your ungrateful head—"

"Ma. I'm talking about Terry, not Dad."

"Oh. Oh god," she gasped. She had gotten pretty shaken over what she thought I'd said. When she heard it was Terry, she cooled right out. "What, you two have a fight or something while we were out?"

I sighed, loudly for her benefit. "Ya, Ma, we had a fight."

"Well, for god's sake, Mick, is that how you solve it, by running away? Come home and straighten it out, instead of acting like . . . like a child."

As she went on, I threw my head back and stared at the ceiling. Then I laid the phone down and stared at it, the little buzzy voice flitting out of it whether I was there or not. I was looking at the old black receiver, heavy and dense like a hammer, I was looking at it and listening to its buzz and hating the hell out of it. My mother's life was full of weak, brutish men, and she'd become expert at not seeing it for what it was. I couldn't change her at this point, but I didn't have to listen to her spin anymore either.

"What kind of a reaction is that, Mick? Did you even hear what I said? I give you the biggest news of all our lives, and you mutter like an insane person."

"Sorry," I said.

"The O'Asis, I said, Mick. We did it, we finally bought it. Everything's going to be different from now on. We talked it over while we were away and first thing Monday we did it. Your father quit his job and everything."

I had by now laid my head down on the telephone table so I could actually hear whatever she said. But it still didn't make any sense.

"Ma, you're joking."

"Well, that wouldn't be a very funny joke now, would it, Mick?"

"No, it isn't," I said.

"So you see, things are already better. Come home, okay? Mick? We want to see you home now. We want to be able to share this now, all of us together."

"*We?*"

"Of course. We all do."

I didn't even bother to go after that one.

"Ma, can you tell me this much? How did the house *smell* when you got home? Did it smell like the regular house smell, or were there maybe other things going on there?"

"Mick, you're acting very weird. I want you home. Now I mean it. You're scaring me."

"No. Humor me, Ma. What did it smell like?"

She waited. She sighed. She said, "Oh Mick, please." She waited some more.

I covered the mouthpiece so she could hear nothing but herself.

"That weekend is over, Mick. It's today now. I want to think about today now, is that all right?"

"What did you smell, Ma?" was my slow response.

"Mick . . . All right, it smelled like dogs. Are you happy? Is that what you ran away from? Is that it, Mick, you ran away from the house because of the dog smell?"

I let it hang there for a long time, because I knew she'd be thinking about it. The disgusting smell of all that went on those two days, the booze and the gas and the dogs and the puke and the honey from Honey. The smell that was coming back to me now like nausea and that I know kicked her right in the nose when she walked through the door because it doesn't go away no matter how hard they scrub or how much carpet cleaner they sprinkle over everything. The smell that she would not talk about, because she didn't talk about that stuff. Fine, Ma, don't talk about it, but here, *remember* it. Smell it again.

"Ya, Ma," I said, worn out from this, "that's what I ran away from. The smell of dog. Listen, I have to go. I gotta get to school. Don't want me to be late for school, do you?"

There was a sort of angry, checkmated tone to her voice. But once again, it was something she wouldn't talk about. "No. Of course I don't. But you come home today, right? After school."

"Gotta run, Ma. I'll see ya," I said, and hung up as she was saying good-bye. I sat there at the telephone table, numbed, confused. I just sat. Sully came out of his room. The phone was right outside his door, and he had probably heard everything.

"Coming?" he asked cautiously.

"Huh? Oh, nah. You go ahead."

Sully left and I continued to sit. His dad came by. "Off the phone, huh? About time."

"Mr. Sullivan?"

"Ya, what is it?"

"I don't have to go to school if I don't want to, do I?"

"Hell no, I ain't your old man. Thank Christ I ain't, too, 'cause if I was your old man, I'd kick your behind, and your brother's too, for the way youse turned out. Then I'd kill my own self. For the same reason."

He stood over me, hands on hips. He smiled. "Any other questions?"

"Nope. Thanks. Got it."

He walked down the stairs, calling back, "No offense, though, Mick."

"Nah," I said.

Honey walked by, looked down at her feet to avoid me, then couldn't help herself, because she's nice. "Good morning, Mick," she said, but hurried on past. This was how it went every time I saw her after the May Day hazing. I was the only male on earth she avoided.

"Where is that idiot paperboy?" I heard Mr. Sullivan growl from downstairs. He seemed to be having fun at the same time he was getting angry. "Ah, here he is." I heard him fling open the front door. "What is there, a Sears bra advertisement in the newspaper today? Every time there's an insert with the Sears bra advertisements you're two hours late with my paper, kid."

I laughed, even though I felt sorry for the kid. Mr. Sullivan made me laugh and I wanted him to go on.

"I got my paper, I'm outta here," he called before slamming the door behind him.

"Doesn't he scare you?" Mrs. Sullivan said from the bottom of the stairs.

"No," I said. "I like him. I'm pretty scare-resistant at this point."

"He scares me," she said. But she was joking. "Come on down here and I'll feed you, truant."

I sat at the small kitchen table in the middle of Mrs. Sullivan's immaculate calico kitchen. All I could say was, "My parents bought the O'Asis." I paused, looked up to her for some comprehension of this tragedy. "*My* parents. Bought a *bar*. Jesus, the hole just gets deeper."

She nodded, placed a plate of sausages and eggs and two buttered English muffins in front of me. "I know," she said, like a sympathy thing. "Sully told me this morning on his way out."

She calls her son Sully, which I love.

I ate like an animal, pounding all that heavy greasy food inside of me as if someone would take it away if I didn't get it all down, now. She seemed to appreciate this, Mrs. Sullivan, as she smiled on me. But my dog-dish style seemed to worry her at the same time.

"She is your mother, Mick," Mrs. Sullivan added. "She's a mother. And I'm certain she's in great pain. You can't just erase it all, your whole life, your people, your background. Can you?"

I'd sure like to find out, is what I wanted to say. But Mrs. Sullivan isn't the kind of person you say stuff like that to. Especially after she's fed you so nice. And I had to admit, I was curious. More than curious. Now that I thought about it, I really wanted to see them, and to see what Terry'd say about the redecoration. If I hid, he still won. I had to show them my smiling, liberated, independent face, and dare Terry to do something about it. I'd whip his ass just by standing up.

"Well, I guess," I said to her, "I guess it doesn't work quite that way, erasing people. Maybe I'll go by and see what's up. As long as I sort of have the day free . . ."

"There you go," she said, brightening up considerably. She felt the way most people felt around here: your family was your family, *no matter what*.

I took the bus to the O'Asis. It is outside of town, but not far outside. To get there from our neighborhood it's a straight twenty-minute bus ride out past the point where neighborhoods mean anything. It sits on a patch of asphalt nowhere, between the city and the oldest and crummiest mall in the area. It's a bus ride my parents have gleefully taken almost every evening—and back again in the wee smalls—for five years, always gooey dreaming of this time, when they could ride the smelly bus to their *own* establishment.

I stepped off the bus—there is a stop right at the door—and stared up at it. The O'Asis. It's sort of a little house with a parking lot and a grotesque pink and green sign spanning the width of the place. "O'Asis" is how it's written. The Irish O', get it? At the front of the words there's an American flag being stuck in the sand by a bunch of marines. At the other end is a palm tree with a leprechaun sitting on top. The whole thing's a little confused.

I took a long breath before walking in. It was like walking backward into night. The place glowed with a low orange-yellow light, and it smelled like things you don't regularly smell in the daytime.

"Now that's my boy," Ma said as she came sweeping out of the back room. She came out around the bar and threw her arms around me. "I knew you'd come back," she said.

Right then I knew: I wasn't coming back.

As she squeezed, my arms remained at my sides. I could not respond to her. What was this hugging about? Do you know what they did to me, Ma? In *your* house? Do you know that I'm homeless, that you're hugging a homeless person?

I felt the strength run out of her grip as she realized she wasn't getting it back. I waited, though I knew it was in vain because when my mother didn't want to see something, she didn't see it. And there was a world of stuff in her life she didn't want to see. Her philosophy always was, when the going gets tough, the tough go to the O'Asis.

It never really bothered me before. It bothered me now. Because I was the victim, and she was my goddamn mother, and that was my goddamn house, and I couldn't go there.

"So, you want to hear what happened?" I said. A formality.

"Terry says to tell you hi," she said, trying to head me off.

"What? What else did he have to say?"

"That was all. Mick, I do wish you'd talk to him. He seems to want to patch things up."

My father walked in from the back, talking on the fly. "After you *stole* from him . . . I'd say that's pretty big of your brother."

I shook my head. "Where is he? Isn't he going to be working with you?"

"Well," Ma said, "we couldn't really have him here . . . ah, we couldn't afford him, is the truth of it. He has steady work anyway, and he should keep it."

I laughed. "You're right, no pub could afford to have Terry on *that* side of the bar."

My father laughed too. Ma wouldn't look at my face. "Oh come on, Mick. You two have had fights before, and you will have fights again. You're brothers. Shake hands and forget about it."

"Ma," I snapped. "You have to hear this."

Then she did turn to me. She looked into my eyes with a more penetrating, knowing stare than I had ever seen before.

"No. I don't," she said, teeth bared like a cornered animal.

She wasn't stupid. She knew a lot. She just wouldn't have it.

Just as quickly, she went back to herself. She turned away and made a grand sweeping gesture over the cramped, dark place.

"Come on, Mick, this is a special time for all of us. Share in it. Let me give you the tour."

I followed her from corner to corner, booth to table. The walls were covered with pictures of fighters who were drunks and politicians who were drunks, all sitting or standing arm in arm with one of the fifty or so previous owners of the place. One corner had two dart boards—on adjoining walls, so that one guy would have to walk into the other guy's line of fire to retrieve his darts. The bubble-topped jukebox had every sickening sappy Irish song ever belched, and there was the world's first video game, Pong, blipping against a wall. Ma beamed at it all.

"Somethin', huh?" my father asked, scanning the place.

"Somethin', Dad."

"You home now?"

I looked at my mother, who looked away.

"No."

He was unmoved, like it was simply a logistical problem. "Well, Jesus, how you gonna live? You gotta take care a y'self, Mick. Listen, I ain't gonna have that sonofabitch Sullivan holding you over my head. That's the only reason he's took ya, y'know, just to stick it to me."

"Gee thanks, make sure you don't leave me *nothin'* there, Dad," I muttered as I turned toward the door.

"What? Hey wait, come back here."

I stopped.

"I ain't kiddin', Mick. You gotta fend for yourself if you ain't at home. Why don't you come work for me?"

It felt like he had waited a long time to make that magnanimous offer to *somebody*, and it just happened to be me.

"I don't think so."

"Can't go on bein' a thief, now can ya," he asked. "You owe your brother some dough, and you're gonna owe Sullivan too. I'll pay ya more to clean up around here than you could make anywhere else. And I'll give you your own key so you can come in and out early, before you have to see any of us, if that's what's botherin' ya."

He had actually thought it out way past me. I was nervous about it, but I saw no holes in the plan. And if I did take it, then it was official—I was out and independent.

"Deal," I said.

"Deal," he said triumphantly. "Come on over here, young man. Belly up and I'll serve ya one on it."

I pushed open the door without looking back at him.

"I already had breakfast, Dad. Leave the keys in the Sullivans' mailbox. I'll be here the next morning."

"You got mail, boy," Mr. Sullivan said. I didn't even see him. The keys just came sailing up the stairs, hung in the air like a skyhook, then dropped to the floor. I scooped them up, along with the note that was stuck in the key ring, curled up like a message in a bottle. "Mick" was written on the outside, in my father's backward-slanted, thick, all-his-weight-on-the-pencil hand-writing. "Six A.M." was all it said inside.

"Mr. Sullivan," I called before he could get away.

"What?" he called back, exasperated, as if I was hounding him all the time. Which I was very careful not to do.

"I want to ask you something."

I heard him sigh from all the way down there. But finally he did come clomping up the stairs.

"Ya, Mick, what is it?" he asked, walking straight over to the refrigerator to check it out. "Good. No booze."

"Right. No booze," I said, just as righteously as he did.

"Ya, that reminds me, Mick, did I hear right? Did your folks buy a *bar*?"

It was my turn to sigh. I did, and nodded.

Mr. Sullivan looked at the floor, half covered his face with his big gorilla hand, and laughed.

"Jesus Christ," he said, still laughing, and shaking his head in amazement. "You wanted to ask me something," he added.

"Ya, well, some *things*, actually. Like, can I decorate this room a little?"

"No nails in the wall," he said.

"Tacks?"

"No."

"Tape?"

"Yes."

"Paint?"

"Ummm . . . hell, no."

"Come on, Mr. Sullivan, I'll do a nice job."

"I'm not buying anything."

"I'm buying."

"Well . . . it better be damn tasteful then, understand?"

"*Damn* tasteful. Space heater?"

"No."

"Hot plate?"

"No."

"Girls?"

He smiled broadly, answered without hesitation. "Certainly, just as soon as we get those balls of yours properly cleavered away, you can have as many as you like."

He watched me as I shifted side to side in my chair. He enjoyed it.

"Anything else, Mick?"

"One more thing. I'm going to pay."

"Pfffft," he said, waving me off as he headed back toward the stairs. "Don't give it a thought." He turned, dripping mock sincerity. "It does my heart good just to know . . . that I'm driving your old man insane."

"No, Mr. Sullivan," I said loud enough to stop him. "I need to do it, okay? For myself. I have a job, I can pay."

"Where'd you get a job?"

I mumbled. "The O'Asis."

"The O—? Your parents' joint?" He shook his head again. "Jesus Christ. I'm smelling you, Mick. Mind me now, I'm taking a good long sniff

183

of you every time you come through that door."

It didn't require a response. He pounded down the stairs alternately laughing and saying "Jesus Christ." I sat there smiling. Nobody had ever smelled my breath before. Nobody had ever told me not to put beer in the fridge. In fact I couldn't remember when anybody had ever told me not to do *anything*. It felt nice, that Mr. Sullivan bothered.

I couldn't *wait* to get a hot plate and girl up there.

Disobedience was the one rush I'd never had before.

Even going to work in the morning was kind of a little thrill. I felt like a man, walking the quiet street at five thirty, coming from *my* place, going to *my* job that would pay for everything. Every day now I owned a little more of myself.

When the bus came close, opened up to take me in, I said hi to the driver, which seemed to shock him. I nodded as I passed each of the other four riders, gloomy and gray and mean as they were, on their way probably to jobs just as crappy as mine but not happy about it like me. It felt like a little club thing we shared silently, bumping along in the rattling filthy bus while most other people were still sleeping. I even said good-bye to the driver as I got off.

I pulled my keys out of my pocket and stuck one in the lock. It was a big dead bolt, a lot of lock, and felt substantial turning in my hand, the tumblers rolling like an airplane propeller inside the door.

I pushed it open, feeling a sense of my power and aloneness.

I yanked the door shut again. There could not exist, anywhere, not in a zoo, not in a cat food factory, a smell as bad as this one. It smelled like my parents' friends.

I stood with my back pressed against the door, hard, as if the smell would try to break out and get me. It wouldn't, of course. The smell was in *there*, and there it would stay. Just it and me.

I had to do it. I threw open the door and rushed inside, as if I could get past it to a spot where it didn't exist. No such. It followed me to the bar, embraced me. I leaned on the bar, closed my stinging eyes, and tried not to breathe. But I had to breathe. After a couple of minutes I worked out a system where I could breathe a few deep breaths, hold it for several seconds, then breathe again. I did this till I got used to the air.

There was twenty dollars in an envelope with

my name on it on the bar. There was a ham sandwich. There was also a list.

> CLEAN THE SHITTER
> MOP FLOORS——USE WAX
> SCRUB BEHIND BAR
> WASH GLASSES IN SINK

Clean the shitter. I put my hands over my
mouth. I knew right away there was no trick to
get me around that one. I went to the broom
room right next to the bathroom and got my
rags and Tilex. For several seconds I stood in
front of the bathroom door unable to move. I
looked at the hanging wooden shingle that said
GALS next to a copy of the old Coppertone ad of a
dog ripping the bathing suit off a girl. It hung
there like a picture on the door. I reached out and
flipped it over. The other side of the shingle said
MEN without any picture. They only had the one
bathroom.

I clenched my teeth and went in with my
Tilex blazing, spraying at everything, trying to
kill whatever foul fungi lurked there. It was
smaller than the broom room, just large enough
for the toilet, the sink, and one body. It smelled
like someone had just used it two minutes ago.
There was a newspaper on the floor.

Like a maniac I sprayed and wiped, sprayed and wiped, the sink, the green tile walls, the floor, the rim of the—

I rushed out of there, to the bar, where I grabbed a glass and a nozzle and pulled myself a Coke. I drank it all down. Waited. I could do this. This would not beat me. I had to do this.

Back into the bathroom, the courage of Coke sizzling in my belly. I scrubbed the rim of the—

I vomited Coke on the floor I'd just cleaned.

But I felt a little better. I cleaned up after myself. Then I cleaned that goddamn toilet.

After a few minutes of sitting on the curb out front with another Coke, I went back in and did the other jobs. Washing the floor was easy, a cup of ammonia and a cup of wax dumped in the water, swabbing the dry wood floor, stacking and unstacking the chairs on top of the little square tables. The rhythm of the squish-squash across the floor was something I liked, and the ammonia in my sinuses was actually kind of a pleasant relief. I washed the eight glasses I found—luckily O'Asis people are the kind who don't mind using the same glass over and over—and scrubbed behind the bar.

The only thing after the bathroom was the floor behind the bar, sticky and chocolate brown from spills of Guiness. It smelled sweet like fruity garbage, and was so gummy I had to use a putty knife to lift it off the floor. When I stood up, the stuff coated my knees, as if I had been working in tar. Shame, Terry's jeans were ruined.

When I was done, I felt good. I felt great. I sat up at the bar, like the bartender, pulled myself another Coke, and ate my sandwich. It was dry and thick, like a small pad of paper between slices of bread, but I enjoyed it. And I couldn't smell anything anymore.

I wrote "Done" on the envelope and marched out the door, locking up.

As I rode the bus to school, I felt powerful. I could do it. This would work. I kept playing with the money in my pocket. This was good money. Much better money than the bag of Terry's bills sitting in the crawl space up in the Sullivans' attic. I wanted to spend it, and I wanted to talk about it. About my job. Not about the shitter and all that, but about the *idea* of my job. And my place. I guess I wanted to talk about me.

I wanted to talk about it with Evelyn Evelyn Evelyn.

Evelyn.

The bus from work brought me to school earlier than usual, so I waited. I paced in front of the building. Some kids started showing up, none of them Evelyn. I went in and hovered around the door to her class, but still nothing. I went back outside to pace in the warm sun.

Everybody else came by. "So, how was first day of work?" Sully asked.

"I cleaned the shitter," I said proudly.

"Super," he said, raising his eyebrows.

"Check it out," I said, spreading the twenty-dollar bill wide like a flag.

"That's nice," he said, truly impressed this time. "Cash every day?"

"Cash every day," I sang.

"Comin' in?"

"Nah, I'm waiting for someone," I said, sounding, I think, like an excited goof.

"Goof," he confirmed, walking in.

"Hey," Toy said as he walked right by me. I started fishing in my pocket for the bill, bouncing to tell him my story, but he kept on walking. I stooped to look up at his face as he brushed past, and he was gone, somewhere else, like he can be sometimes for no good reason. That's when you leave him alone.

I was getting angry by the time Ruben came slinking by.

"*Where* is Evelyn?" I demanded, which was a stupid move because demanding at Ruben only made him less helpful.

"Who?"

"Evelyn, your sister. She's never this late. Where is she?"

"I ain't got no sister Evelyn. I got a sister Magdalena."

"Where is she?"

"Lena?"

"Ya, Lena, all right? Where is she?"

"She's at home. She's sick."

He disappeared into the school. As I stood on the wide steps alone, the bell clanged, like a fire alarm, to start classes. I felt all that energy I had run right out of me, down through my feet, down over the steps to the street as I trudged into the building.

School took an eternity that day, but I got through it by playing over and over in my head the story of my independence as I'd sing it to Evelyn.

Ringing and ringing on Evelyn's doorbell. The monster dog barked from the backyard. I barked back at him.

"What are you, *mental*?" Evelyn snarled, throwing open her door. Her hair stood a foot out from her head in every direction. She tied a giant yellow shoelace around the waist of her frayed plaid flannel bathrobe and yanked the lace tight, angrylike. She was greenish pale, like a kiwifruit.

"You look so beautiful," I slobbered.

"I'm lying *down* here, Mick. Home *sick, tú sabes*?"

It would not matter what she said to me. I puffed up, folded my hands formally, and let them hang in front of my crotch.

"I am a man of means now, Evelyn, independent. So I've come to ask you for a proper date." I shut up and waited.

"Let me smell your breath." She broke down and smiled a little.

"Jesus," I said, "what's with the smelling my breath lately? It's getting real popular." It pissed me off, this suggestion that I'd have to keep being suspected for the old shit.

I rushed up, aggressively, and blew in her face. "Good enough?"

She winced. "Well no, it still isn't honey-suckle. But it's a good healthy stink."

"So it's a date then."

"Slow down now. What are we talking about, like, a real date where you spend money and treat me right, stuff like that?"

"Exactly," I yelled. It sounded even greater when she described it.

"Not interested."

"What?" I started hyperventilating. "Whaddya mean? I just want to . . . I only mean . . . what I'm trying to say . . ."

"Hold it," she laughed. "Take it slowly now, speak clearly, that's the boy."

I took a deep breath. "I want you to come and see my place. It's not a big deal or anything, but . . . it's nice. And I'm fixing it up to be nicer. And it's mine. I want to show it to you, that's all. I'll cook for you. You know, dinner. I'll cook you dinner, at my place."

"Well," she said, "you make quite a compelling pitch, I'll say that. My head is turned."

It sure sounded good, but I wasn't taking any chances. "Um, 'Head is turned,' that would be a yes. Yes?"

"Yes."

Grinning like a monkey I backed down the stairs. Evelyn shook her head at me, but looked pleased all the same.

"What's gotten into you?" she asked.

I pointed at her. "I have looked into the future, and my future is *you*."

She winced, like something hurt her. Maybe her sickness. "I don't know, maybe you should go take another look," she said.

I was shaking my head no when I backed into Ruben coming up the stairs.

"Yo, *chico*," he said. "Get outta here. We don't need no freakin' cyclopedias."

Table for One

"**I**s there a table around here I can use, Sul?"

"So she's actually coming up here?"

"Actually."

He bent over to look under the bed he was sitting on, and dragged a folding card table out. He flipped it open.

"Great," I said. "Check it out."

Like a magician I swirled the tablecloth around my body, flapped it in the air, and brought it down over the table. The cloth was cream color, with a little lace trim all around the edges and so many perfectly circular wine or grape-juice glass stains that it looked like a pattern. It was also about eight times the size of the tabletop, and hung on the floor all around. It cost a dollar at the thrift shop. I set down two tall twenty-five-cent wineglasses at either end, mismatched dishes, stainless steel service for two, and two candle-holders shaped like the Bunker Hill monument that were so sharp looking I forked over two bucks for them. I stuck in the black candles, stood back, and admired.

"We can fold the tablecloth smaller," he said, stroking his chin.

"Sure," I said, "sure, we can do that," all ner-vous like I *needed* his approval. I was happy he was finally coming around to support me in this.

He pointed at the wineglasses and looked at me with eyebrows raised. "For vino?" he asked.

"Well, ya, I thought, maybe . . ."

He made the *tsk-tsk* noise, but went on. "Servin' sandwiches, Mick?"

A big smile overtook my face. I pulled out my big score, the four-dollar commercial hot plate big enough to warm a whole pizza. I held it up by its ancient, unraveling, cloth-covered cord.

"You know what my old man thinks about that."

"You gonna rat?"

"No, this could be fun. I never seen my old

man actually off a guy before. Only heard him talk about it. But you can't really cook nothin' on that, can you?"

"I think I can make a soup. A real one I mean, with big pieces of meat and cut-up vegetables and all that."

He nodded at me, nodded, nodded, looked over my table setup. "Mick, you can't serve soup on flat plates. It'll run over the sides. Then it'll roll off the table, through the floor, onto my father's dome, and he'll come up here, see you have alcohol, a hot plate, a babe *and* that you're doing witchcraft, and he'll shoot you down dead like a dog. So flat plates won't do."

"Shut up, I know that. They didn't have any down at the thrifty. I'll get some."

Sully put up his hands. "Okay, I didn't mean to insult your stuff. Really, Mick, I think this is real nice. Come Saturday, I think she's yours."

"Don't be smutty," I said. "But really, you think so?" I practically jumped, as if *Sully* had promised me something.

"I don't see how she can resist."

Sully slipped away down the stairs, and in a minute he was back. Or at least his hand was. He reached up through the bannister and slipped two soup bowls sideways between the rails. "We

195

never have soup downstairs. But don't break them just the same."

"Thanks," I said and got no reply.

I found my father sleeping on the floor behind the O'Asis bar.

"Dad, you make it kind of hard for me to do my job, with you lying there in the gunk I have to scrape up."

He groaned, pushed himself up, and started explaining as if it was no big deal. He seemed to believe it too.

"I slept there before, y'know, it's no big deal."

I dropped to my knees to start scrubbing. His big head fell into his small hands. Then he popped up again.

"Hey, get me something, Mick."

He didn't elaborate, and I didn't think about it much before spinning around and pouring a double Wild Turkey. I did it all in one motion, slick as any full-time bartender. I brought it out to him, then listened to the rest of the story from scrubbing position on the floor behind the bar.

"Well no, I take that back," he said, as he slammed the heavy glass down on the tabletop. "I never slept *there* before. I slept *there*, and I slept over *there*." I figured he was pointing around the room, but it didn't matter enough to either of us for me to stand up and look. "But I never slept there, behind the bar before." There was a certain amount of pride in his words. "You know why, Mick? Because it wasn't *mine* before. Now, when I want to, I get to sleep behind *my* bar." He thumped himself twenty times hard on the sternum as he said it.

"And at least now," he said, "when I wake up, I'm already to work." He laughed robustly at his own joke before adding, "And your mother will get over it. She always comes around."

"That's great, Dad," I said.

He practically climbed the bar over me to reach the bottle. He grabbed it and disappeared again.

Since it was a Saturday, the place was extra messy, and it took longer to clean. I had to work fast. My father was gracious enough to stay clear as he watched me work. When I came from behind the bar to start the floor, he moved to the opposite side of the room. When I reached that side, he moved to a stool at the bar. Wherever he went he took his bottle and glass with him. It wasn't real drinking, though, not nighttime-style drinking. It was recovery, hair-of-the-dog drinking, which he believed in wholeheartedly. This type of drinking he'd stop by opening time, and not have another until dinner usually. And except for the smell of his breath and pores, and the cheeriness, the average person could not tell that he'd had a drop.

Just before I got to the bathroom swab, Dad went in. A little while later he came out, and I went in.

I came staggering back out and collapsed at a table. He brought me a Coke there, served it at my table like I'd done for him. "Sorry about that." He shrugged.

"Not a problem," I said, downing the Coke and finishing my filthy disgusting job.

I put everything away in the closet, approached the bar. "Gotta get paid, Dad," I said, very businesslike.

"Course ya do, course ya do," he said, fumbling at the cash register. He was still at that bottle, longer than I figured he would be. He pressed buttons all over the register, swore at it, slapped it, and it opened. Stuck his hand in like a bear snagging a fish out of a stream, whirled, and pushed the money on me. It was forty dollars.

"I never seen ya work before, Mick. Ya do good. Fast and thorough. You're good."

I took it and nodded. I just wanted to go. Somehow I was always extra humiliated when he tried to be nice to me.

"Can I have some wine?" I blurted.

"Indeed?" he said, joking like to scold me. But really he seemed pleased. He started drawing a glass from an already tapped bottle.

"No, Dad, no. I don't mean I want some now. I mean, can I have a bottle? For later."

He deflated. "Why should I? *Boy.*"

"I got a date tonight. A nice date. A dinner thing."

He smiled. He leered, actually, but I ignored that because I wanted something from him.

"What's your best wine, Dad? Something classy, 'cause this is a really classy girl."

"André. Cold duck. Pink." He gave me a knowing wink. "Trust me on this. I am a saloon keeper, you know." He said the phrase *saloon keeper* like it meant Sun God or something.

He was so full of pride, finally with his chance to share his brand of fatherly wisdom. He stuck an arm deep into the beer chest and pulled out a bottle. "Girls love the shit out of it," he said. He pulled out a second bottle and stood it next to the first. "Take two. That's twice as classy."

I thanked him and held out some money as he fumbled around back there for a big enough bag.

"Get that out of here," he said, pushing my

hand away. I nodded, took my bag, and headed for the door.

"Where ya goin'?" he said sadly. "Opening ain't for twenty minutes yet, can't ya stay, just with me? The whole damn joint all ours, for a while?"

It almost sounded nice, the way he said it. I wished it was for real. But then I remembered the drinking he'd already done. The niceness was an accident. And any minute, it would be gone.

"Sorry, Dad, I can't. Have to get back and fix up my place for tonight."

"*Your place*," he mimicked me, nasty, because he had to pull me back down below him before I got away. That was just his way, that swing from sappy and nice to small and mean. It didn't bother me much anymore though. "Go on then, go to *your place*, your little place. I'll stay here, 'cause this here is *My Place*."

As I quickly locked the door from the outside, three people crowded me, already lined up for opening time at His Place. Two skinny guys with sunglasses sandwiching an older lady in black eye makeup, like an outfielder in a day game.

I went to the store. I bought a little sample bottle of aspirin because I was getting a headache already. A Cornish game hen because I couldn't find a real chicken small enough. Carrots, celery, green beans. I brought my stuff up to the girl at the register and mentioned what I was making. She sent me back for a can of chicken broth, a tiny box of Bell's seasoning, pasta elbows, and chickpeas.

Back at home, I went to work. Plunked the bird into the broth mixed with water and set it on the hot plate. The pot I had was big for the plate, kind of like one of the fat Cormac brothers sitting on a bar stool. But I figured the heat would get up there eventually. After the chicken cooked for about an hour I added the chopped-up vegetables and the spice. I could smell it now, and it smelled warm and clingy, like stuff I'd sometimes whiff from downstairs in the Sullivans' kitchen. I opened the two windows to let it out.

It made me sleepy, that homey smell, but I was jumpy. I lay down on the bed. My eyes kept springing open. I stared at the ceiling. I closed my eyes but only got more nervous. I got up and stirred the pot.

I fell asleep finally after walking from the bed to the pot and back for the third time. I had a short dream, like a quick-cut music video flashing black-and-white images of my father sleeping on the floor. I woke up disgusted, disappointed, tired, and shaking with nerves.

I went downstairs and took a shower, came back up, paced, stirred the pot, dumped in a half pound of pasta, sweated like an animal, took another shower.

I felt as if so much of my life, my new life, had come to depend on this date, and the pressure was withering me. I dressed in a gathering cloud of gloom, certain that I was going to speak nothing but babbles to Evelyn. I had to calm down or explode.

Slowly, yet desperately, I started the walk. Across the room, a mile or so. I pulled the chilled cold duck from the refrigerator.

No corkscrew, damn. No corkscrew, damn. I got a steak knife, stabbed the bottle in the head, twisted the knife, rocked it, churned it, until the cork was sliced and ground up, some pieces pulling up when I extracted the knife, more of them floating in the wine.

Just a glass.

Just a glass.

I should not be worried. This is better. This is fine.

I stirred the soup.

And I'm a good cook.

I have a job. I am a man. I don't need anything, and that is a good thing.

When I checked again, the pasta elbows were swelled to the size of copper plumbing joints. I turned the hot plate down to low. It smelled wonderful.

Good thing there was a second bottle of duck.

I stood weaving on Evelyn's porch. Three pokes of my finger, and I hit the doorbell. I giggled. That was when the door opened.

Evelyn stood in the doorway in a long, electric blue sort of peasant dress, with ruffles on the shoulders and a whole village of people embroidered all the way around the hem. Her hair was pulled back in a long tight braid. She looked for the first time defenseless and soft and hopeful.

For about three seconds. The broad white smile she brought to the door fell away as she sized me up.

"You're drunk?" she asked. "You come to me drunk?"

"Nah," I said shaking my head desperately. "No, I'm not. I had . . . I had . . . I had a wine." I shrugged.

"You had a *wine*," she said, nodding slowly. "You had a wine, eh, Mick? Look at me, dammit." She yanked at her skirt. "How often do you think I do this nonsense, huh?"

I started to answer.

"I had *hope*, here, Mick. I had hope for this, hope for you. I don't *do* this, you understand?" She stepped out onto the porch, and ripped my face with a loud, ringing slap.

"You come to me drunk? What do you think, I'm some kind of *puta* here? That you can do this? Get out of here."

By the time she hit me, I was glad she hit me.

"Go ahead," I said quietly. "Hit me again if you want to."

"No. You'll probably like it." She still seemed totally amazed at something that never amazed anyone before—me showing up gassed. "Who do you think you *are*?"

It was like she was a cop asking to see my driver's license, when I knew I'd been driving without one. I scrambled, but I had nothing to show her.

"I don't know. Evelyn. I don't know who I am at all. I need to be told. Like, before, before, I had an identity. The identity sucked, but at least I had one. To not have one . . . it's like a weird little hell thing. Now I'm up there in my place, you know, and, like, there's nothing. I don't hear nothing, don't see nothing, don't feel nothing that reminds me who I am. I don't even have a mirror up there 'cause I'm half afraid I'll look in it and not see anything. I need to be told."

She stood with her hands on her hips. I saw, briefly, in her smart, gentle face, a softening. I knew she understood. Then she stiffened.

"You looking for sympathy here? There is *ninguno*. Go."

She stomped inside and slammed the door.

The desperation in me was so real it felt like I'd swallowed something live and it was clawing around in my belly.

I knocked. The mail slot opened.

"Go home and sleep, Mick." The mail slot closed.

I knocked again, my hand half open, the way drunks do. "I don't want to go back there alone, Evelyn. I need help."

She opened the door one more time, leaned on the door frame like she was suddenly very tired. "You certainly do," she said. "But I'm sorry, Mick, I just can't be taking care of you. We all have our own stuff, you know? You're not a whole person. You've got to get right."

"I'll be better." I sounded like such a simp, I even surprised myself. "This won't happen again. It wasn't my fault . . ."

She put up her hands. "Stop that now, I'm embarrassed just listening to you. You are responsible for yourself, that much I know. As long as you want to believe somebody else is responsible, you're going to be useless. You really want my advice, I say go on back home. Not to Sully's, but to your real home. You think you're not them, and that's your problem."

She had me on the ropes now, and she just wouldn't let me fall down. I was good and beaten.

"That's bullshit," I snapped, effectively ending the conversation.

"Good luck, Mick," she said before closing the door for good. "I really mean that." It hurt all the more because she really did mean it.

I stood in the dark outside my parents' house, staring at it. The second bottle of cold duck filled my belly and my head and my bones. But it hadn't put me down, put me away like it was supposed to. So I came back out and stood staring in the dark, rolling my tongue in and out and in and out, trying to shake the tiny flecks of cork off it.

All the lights were off. I shuffled up the front steps, stood for a while more in front of the door. Finally I stuck my key in. It jammed. The lock didn't turn. I pulled the key out, turned it over, and tried again. Nothing. Then I noticed, the lock was new.

"I changed it," Terry hissed, *right* in my ear.

My terror came out in tears rolling down the creases alongside my nose.

"Kill me, Terry. Go ahead. 'Cause if it was me, if I get the chance, I'm gonna kill you."

He spun me around by the shoulders to face him.

"You're drunker den me," he said, beaming.

"Well, do something," I said.

"Good to see ya back in the old form, Mickey."

"Shut up and take your shot."

It didn't matter what I said. He had his script ready.

"By the way, *great* move, pissing in my Bushmills, Mick. I been waitin' ta see ya so I could tell ya: That's just what I woulda done. When I saw that, I knew you was gonna be all right. Hear me? *That's just what I woulda done.*"

I closed my eyes. "Hit me, asshole. Kill me."

He laughed. "If I blow on ya, you'll fall down."

"So blow me," I said.

He reached over me, stuck his key in the shiny new lock, and opened the door. Like a doorman, he gestured toward the inside and said, "Comin' in, Mick?"

"No way," I muttered. "Came to *kill* your ass. If you don't kill me first."

"Ain't gonna," he said. "I'm feelin' magfuck-innanimous tonight. And, I got new hope for ya, boy. I'm givin' ya time. You'll be back wit us, I know it. And when you come, I'll take ya."

He smiled at me, the sickest snaggle-tooth victory grin.

"Sure you won't come in?" he asked.

I shook my head dumbly, but as defiantly as I could manage.

Terry went in the house, used the phone, went to the refrigerator, and came out with two beers. I took one. "I'd walk ya home, buddy, but your new landlord keeps promisin' ta accidentally blow my brains out if I'm near his house in the dark. Y'understand."

When the cab came, Terry put me in it. He gave the driver the Sullivans' address and he paid him with his own money. Then he leaned in and gave me a filthy, stinko kiss on the forehead.

"See, ain't I nice?" he asked before telling the driver to take off.

Hermit Crab

I had just a little bit of a dream, of being in the woods with the Scouts, me and Sully, and Baba was there even, back when people still called him Ryan because he wasn't yet teenage wasteland, and he was eating the legs off a live frog he caught with a long homemade frog sticker. Campfire was burning, crackling loud and broken up with the occasional little explosion of a pinecone. There was no other sound at all, and it was soothing, warming my whole front until I turned myself around and warmed my whole back, and that strange forceful fire sound making me feel bigger inside. We stood around, kids all of us, just kids, smiling at the fire and leaning too close so that our already red faces got cracky with the dry heat, which was okay enough. Even Baba, who was still Ryan.

And there wasn't another sound but that fire sound, no dopey guitar or camping songs, no fart contests, no big hog–little hog jokes. Fire sound alone.

Until the blast of a whooshing tornado noise ripped through it.

I jumped up in bed, stood there on my knees, watching Mr. Sullivan working the small kitchen fire extinguisher. The last of the yellow flame lapped up the wall behind the hot plate before finally it was all squirted out.

I knew that I had done something horrible, that I had left the stupid soup on all night and had set a fire in the place where they took me in.

Mr. Sullivan threw the extinguisher down on the floor with a crash, then stood staring at me with his hands on his hips. He didn't talk right off, just stood, and stared, melting me hotter and quicker than if he'd let the flame get me.

"Should have let the flame get you," he growled. "You're lucky I have a nose like a damn dog."

He looked massive, much bigger than ever before, his mustache bushier and whiter over his fire-reddened face. I shook, could see myself shaking, as I waited for the beating.

It was five minutes. He stared at me. I shook and I shook. I tried to stop it, to get hold of myself, but it got worse, more noticeable until the whole bed was trembling in the corners of my eyes. I was petrified to turn away, so he just burned that stare into me. He looked like a thing carved out of stone. His big chest didn't move with breathing, his eyes didn't water, his obscene pointed Adam's apple didn't hitch once. It was a beating, what he did to me with his presence.

Then he was done. "You want to ask me if I'm surprised?" he asked coldly.

"I don't, Mr. Sullivan."

"I'm afraid you're just genetically wired to be a waste, Mick. I suppose it ain't your fault, but . . ." He walked out banging two giant fists together hard, leaving me with the mess, the smoke, and the chemical stench of the snuffed fire, and with myself.

I fell right over on my nose as soon as he was gone, toppled right off the side of the bed and didn't have the strength to raise my hands to shield my face. I lay there flat-faced for a second, thought about it all, then banged my forehead on the floor on purpose. I did it again. I did it again and again and again and again.

Then I packed my stuff, as much as I could get into one bag, and slithered out. No one else in the house was up yet. I didn't know where Mr. Sullivan was, which made me run all the way down the stairs and out the door.

I stopped running when I was a block away. On my way to where? I was still chewing crumbs of cork and gummy soup as I thought about my whereabouts. Nowhere. Where was my home? On my back, like a hermit crab. In the pack with a few pairs of Terry's pants and the last of the stolen money, also from Terry. I had stopped running, but still walked briskly. No reason for that. I stopped, sat on the curb.

"I ain't genetically wired for nothin'," I said. I winced when I recalled having a beer with Terry the night before. "Bullshit, bullshit. I don't have nothing to do with them, they have nothing to do with me . . ." I opened the pack and started pulling the clothes out, flinging pants here, shirts there, all over the deserted street. Then the money. Terry's one-dollar bills, crumpled into wads like baseballs, thrown as far as I could. I tipped the bag upside down, laughed hard as the last of everything fell to the ground and I threw the bag too.

"I'm free, I'm clean. I'm the freest guy in the goddamn world." I sat on the curb to watch the bills blow around. "Everybody wishes they were me now. The free guy, they'll call me." I put my elbows on my knees, there on the curb, and my face in my hands.

There wasn't much wind. Only one car went by. The money really didn't blow. The clothes certainly didn't go anywhere. It was all still there in front of me when I lifted my face out of the little puddle I'd made in my palms.

I went into the street and picked up my bag. I moved around like a pathetic little old man as I collected everything back up again.

Standing outside Toy's house later that Sunday morning, I wasn't quite sure what to do. I had used up every other option. Maybe this time he'd take me on a permanent road trip far, far away from here.

I didn't want to ring the bell, so I threw pebbles. Four throws, two hits, no answer. Three more hits, no answer. One big clank, thought I cracked the window, thought about running.

Felina appeared in the window. Of course I hit the wrong window. I started backing away, mouthing, "Sorry, sorry," and bowing like a servant as I did.

She didn't respond in any way. She just kept

staring, expressionless. First I thought she was angry, but then I didn't think so. I stopped backing off. I stared back. I supposed I was quite a sight by then, but it couldn't have been all that interesting to her. She had me locked with her eyes. She held up a hand for me to wait.

I met her at the door. She was wearing red cutoff sweatpants and a thin white muscle T-shirt with straps instead of sleeves.

"Toy's not here," she said.

"Oh. Road trip, right?" I said, trying, and failing, not to stare at her. A small morning breeze blew by, and she folded her arms.

"Carlo's not here, either," she said.

"I'm sorry. I shouldn't have woken you up. This is really stupid of me. I don't know what I'm doing lately."

"You're limping again. Like last time."

I had to smile, because that felt good—the connection to before, the idea that she noticed something about me. I looked down at my legs, bounced on them, leaning on the left, then the right. "I don't think so," I said.

"The psychic limp, I mean. You always come dragging into this port."

"Ya," I said, holding the dopey smile. "I seem to, huh? Well, you did tell me, that other time, that I should come back again."

Finally, she smiled a different kind of smile. Not an "I know things" smile that made me blush and that made me feel sad for her, but a "this is nice" smile. "Then it's an invitation you're responding to here, in the wee hours of a Sunday morning. I see." She paused long enough for me to get nervous. "So I should let you in then."

"No," I snapped, for no other reason than that was the very last thing I *wanted* to say and that's the way my brain was working. My brain, my whole body, was so overloaded at that moment, fizzing and zapping like a radio dropped into a bathtub full of water.

Felina stepped back, looking deeply embarrassed. She looked at the floor, looked behind her. "I'm sorry, you're right, I'm sorry. It's just . . . anyway, it's not your problem."

Her sudden frailty, that retreat into a sad and naked neediness, surprised me. I loved finding it, like I'd met an old friend. It made me feel somehow like I had a right to be here.

"What I meant was yes," I rushed, before she could regroup.

She smiled broadly, still looking down a bit to hide it.

"You sure this isn't a mistake?" I asked cautiously, giving her a fair chance to wake up.

"Oh, I'm certain that it is," she said. "But you know there are rules. Like in the Dracula movies where Dracula can't come in your house unless you invite him in. I know the rules, I know the risks, so it's my own fault what happens to me, isn't it?" Her voice had regained the snap and confidence, which didn't intimidate me so much, now that I had heard the other.

"Right, Dracula?" she asked as she took my hand and led me inside.